CREATURES

For Robin

CREATURES

A NOVEL

Crissy Van Meter

ALGONQUIN BOOKS OF CHAPEL HILL 2020

Published by
ALGONQUIN BOOKS OF CHAPEL HILL
Post Office Box 2225
Chapel Hill, North Carolina 27515-2225

a division of
WORKMAN PUBLISHING
225 Varick Street
New York, New York 10014

LIBRARY OF CONGRESS CATALOGING-IN-PUBLICATION DATA

Names: Van Meter, Crissy, author.
Title: Creatures / a novel by Crissy Van Meter.
Description: First edition. | Chapel Hill, North Carolina :
  Algonquin Books of Chapel Hill, 2020.
Identifiers: LCCN 2019010469 | ISBN 9781616208592
  (hardcover : alk. paper)
Classification: LCC PS3622.A5854948 C74 2020 | DDC 813/.6—dc23
LC record available at https://lccn.loc.gov/2019010469

10 9 8 7 6 5 4 3 2 1
First Edition

For Dana

An island can be dreadful for someone from outside.
Everything is complete, and everyone has his obstinate,
sure, and self-sufficient place. Within their shores,
everything functions according to rituals that are as
hard as rock from repetition, and at the same time
they amble through their days as whimsically and
casually as if the world ended at the horizon.

—TOVE JANSSON, *The Summer Book*

To me the sea is a continual miracle,
The fishes that swim—the rocks—the motion of the waves—
the ships with men in them,
What stranger miracles are there?

—WALT WHITMAN, "Miracles"

CONTENTS

CREATURES

Hypothesis—

What fills the space: water, sky, land, air.

THURSDAY

There is a dead whale. It rolls idly in the warm shallows of this island, among cartoonish sea animals with tentacles, suction cups, and goopy eyes. There are squawking birds leaking nearly colorless shit, and we are concerned with an unbearable odor and the must-be sharks circling nearby.

This whale is lodged in the half-moon of the bay, and she can't seem to drift past the reef, even with the water pushing out. Close enough that we can see her. We can smell her. We breathe her. She moves with the comings and goings of the tides, and her lifeless body is a black balloon on the horizon. The smell has seeped into this house and lingers in the curtains. Rancid stench sticks to the ends of my hair. In the night, there are sea voices—chewing into her carcass—and when I can't sleep, I can make out the blubber plucked by night beaks and mouths of darkness unknown. Some mornings, her dead eye has been opened wide, and others, she's capsized and looks like the hull of a boat.

There isn't time for this now.

I rush to the harbor, where men are heaving fish from boats to bloodstained docks and piling them in silvery mountains on top of crushed ice. It smells familiar. The air is wet and moves deep into the lungs, and today, I'm frantic. I ask about Liam's boat, if it has come back, if anyone has seen him.

"You seen that whale out there in the bay?" they keep asking.

"Storm's still out there, Evie, and we heard they're still trying to get around it," they say.

"You don't worry one minute," they say.

"We lost all radio contact last night. Happens all the time," they say.

I'm used to guts, stink, men who drink, boats, island gossip, and sudden darkness that fills the sky. I know that storms sometimes appear unexpectedly, and I know that there are times when we have predicted them for years. I know the maze of floating docks covered in a slimy layer of raspberry-colored insides, and I know which fishermen work with efficient, tenacious speed. There is never time to waste.

The men load a crate of fresh dead fish into my truck, and I pretend I'm not worried—that I'm an old seaman, too—that this weekend will be fine, that Liam will be back in time for our wedding, that I'll be able to gut, cut, and prep all this fish alone. He always comes back. I keep saying that. And everything always smells like fish here.

The sky is filled with gray clouds pissing rain, and as I get closer to home, I can see the outline of that rotten whale and the infinite outline of that infinite storm. I tell myself to stop thinking of the whale, to think of Liam instead, but there it is, right there.

Tires are slower in the mud, and my truck slips in the gravel driveway, and I can't lose this haul of fish, because what if the boats never come back? The most important thing now: get the tuna into the freezer. I say it out loud: *Tuna to the freezer.*

But there is my mother, standing on my porch. Holding her hand up with an awkward wave. It's been years. Her eyes are the same, dark and eager. I'm soaked, and she's dry. Then she points to the horizon, to warn me of the beached whale lingering on the reef, or to warn of darkness.

My mother has a sensitive nose. She could be burned at the stake for this gift. She can smell pizza before a delivery guy gets out of the car. When I lost my virginity, she said she could *smell* it on me. She says she can still smell my father. All the things she can smell, they draw her to new places, and maybe it's her heightened senses that are the root of our problems. Sometimes she's near, sometimes she's not, and sometimes she says that she can smell when I need her by a tinge of smoke in the air. This dead-whale perfume is polluting the entire leeward side of Winter Island, and it's beginning to seep into the cracks of my skin. But it's not the worst thing to happen to us.

Today, I do not want to see my mother, because today, she will compare everything to this rotting whale. Our lives. Our sadness. Our dead. I haven't seen her in three years. Haven't heard her voice in two. And haven't received a letter in at least six months, but here she is, waving and pointing. Like she's the first to discover the body of a whale.

"Can you help me get the tuna into the freezer in the garage?" I ask.

"That's how you greet your mother?" she asks.

But I didn't know you were coming, I should have said. (And other things.)

I walk to her, rain-covered, fish-covered, and kiss her on the cheek. She backs away slowly, about to tell me what she smells. I'm about to say I always smell this way, and she musters up glassy eyes to make me feel something. She always wants me to *feel* something. I'm about to say that I'm just all guts anyway.

"You must have known I'd be here for your wedding," she says.

HER NAILS ARE acrylic and red, like her mother's were, and she's inside my house, touching everything with the plastic tips of her fingers: Organizing stacks of mail on the dining table, rearranging my spice rack. She's checking for dust and grime.

She nears my face and holds my chin in her fingertips, and she tells me I'm flushed.

"That fire is warm," I say.

"You're nervous," she says. "Cold feet."

There is a blanket of white fog. We can barely make out the vast green fields from the windows, but still my mother says she can make out the mound of the whale's belly if she squints her eyes at the shoreline. She keeps checking the window, pinching her nose, while the whale is teetering out there, rising and falling like the ocean is gasping long breaths. She points to a planter of dead flowers and then out to sea.

"How can we have a wedding with that thing out there?" she asks.

It was a mistake to tell her about Liam. About my life. It was a mistake to think she wouldn't make things worse. Most everything with her is always a mistake. She's nitpicky about my garden, the whale, the fog, everything. I could tell her what I really think of her or, at least, what I think of her nails.

"You shouldn't have planted those roots so early," she says.

Roses are nestled in beds that trace the perimeter of my house. I tell her I want to be buried right beneath them.

"They are so full this year," I say.

She's rustling through my cupboards and makes no remark on their emptiness. My mother has always arrived unannounced and quick to tell you what she thinks. About anything. Her moments of empathy are fleeting, and I've never figured out why and how they appear. Maybe sorcery. She's never been much of a mother, because she left me with Dad, and the times she did come back to this island, she offered pockets full of eclectic toys and trinkets, and then left within days, sometimes hours. It was awful to watch him love her so much, especially because she's so lovable sometimes.

There's not much to do here but stare at the sea.

"You and your father love the damn ocean more than anyone," she says.

I don't know what my mother eats, what kinds of foods she buys these days, where she lives, or how she got here. I know that in the 1990s, she was on diets and refused bread. There was a time when there was no dairy. Another when it was meat only.

I offer her my bread.

"I made it myself," I say. "Liam and I love to cook."

She cuts cucumbers and carrots. She talks about the mountain garden patch she kept that was infested with insects, which ate her radishes dead. Then, more about the wedding. She keeps talking—she fills all the empty space with stories—and I am silent, talking in nods, smirks, and knife cuts.

The last of today's sun is breaking through the fog, and it seems like the worst of things might pass. There is light in the kitchen. The fiery glow illuminates the walls. We agree without speaking that we should go outside, as if we can't help it, to enjoy the remaining light. She finds an old bottle of wine in the pantry and pours it into two mugs. I tell her I'm allergic, and she laughs. I say sorry for no wineglasses. I try to tell her there's a deadly storm at sea.

"That's fucking ridiculous," she says.

"It's been out there for days," I say.

"I mean, you are not allergic to wine," she says.

"It makes my ears burn and my face red," I say.

"You're just nervous."

A deer prances on the lawn, looks us in the eye, and bounces away. The dogs, guilty and muddy, return from a day of wandering, and I embrace them on the porch. My mother is hesitant about the outside smell, the dirty dogs, and apparently other things, but I can tell she's at least trying. The big dog jumps up and plants his paws on her chest, and she smiles through it, but her teeth are so tight they might shatter. My mother here helps me forget that Liam could be at the bottom of the sea or, worse, that he's chosen never to return to me.

I grab a beer from the cooler on the porch.

"You and your father really love your beer," she says.

We eat more bread, and I throw a stick on the lawn for the dogs. We are restless and hungry, and there is still light.

"You must just get used to this smell," she says.

Notfuckingusedtothissmelljesusfuckingchrist.

With a mouthful of bread, I ask her nicely what the fuck she means.

"You know, the ocean, it just smells so bad. That's the one thing I couldn't live with," she says.

Winter Island is a mound of volcanic rock half-carved by glaciers, full of lush green forests and sweeping sandy beaches. There are steep cliffs that crumble from eternities of erosion. There have been woolly mammoths. There have been settlers left behind, and we know, because we spend money and years digging them out of the dirt. Mainlanders say our island was settled by trolls, the Spanish, and then all the lonely people. Our marijuana claims magical powers. Mostly sunshine. Forty miles from Los Angeles on a scenic ferry ride with room for cars and concessions. There are plenty of reasons to stay.

MY MOTHER IS drinking fast, and she's telling me about the things in wine that might make me allergic. I don't have the courage to tell her any truth, like, *I already know about tannins.* Like, *I am no idiot.* Like, *I am a grown woman with a beating heart, and skin, and nails, and happiness, and anger.* That I don't want her at the wedding. That it's not even a wedding, but a yard party, with fish, and fisher-men, and all the sea smells. I won't tell her about the red roses I'll put in my hair.

She encourages me to try more wine. This is how it goes with her—there's no *no*.

I need air. Even if it's polluted with dead-whale rot. I am stomping around the muddy yard with bare feet, I touch the petals of the roses with care, and I try to enjoy the lingering glow left after the last moments of sun.

My mother shouts from the porch and suggests I get gar-den Crocs, and that I should really figure out what to do with the whale.

The whale smell *is* almost unbearable, but I will never admit it. I walk around the yard concerned only with how damp the soil will be for the wedding, pushing my feet into soft spots and estimating how long they'll take to dry. The thing about bays: It's easy to get trapped in the swooping curve of their bellies, and there are only small mouths to let everything out. All exits must be planned with care. It's possible to be trapped inside a bay forever.

My mother can't stand the smell, she tells me again, and slithers inside. She can find things that aren't even there. She will.

She is walking around the living room. Her clothes hang on her like sails. Her loose sleeves are dangerously close to the flames. She tosses wood into the fireplace, and the house smells of crisp cedar and birch wood. Less dead carcass now.

She sits next to me on the couch and sinks her back deep into a pile of pillows. She's almost too close as she tells me about a cooking class she took in New York City.

"Oh, you would just hate that place, Evie," she says.

I feel uneasy near the warmth of her skin, the heat of the fire, and the fire inside from all the booze. I want her love, but I want to hit her, too. Sometimes I have the urge to lean my head against her shoulder, but I fight it, because like her, she says I'm *one hell of a fucking fighter*.

"The teacher was really French, and we made the best beef bouillon."

But she's really here to tell me I've made a mistake. To question my decisions. She hasn't come out and said it yet. She wants to tell me that Liam won't understand, or that he'll never make me happy. She'll tell me I barely know him, and that I shouldn't have rushed into this, and that he's not really an island person. Not like my father, and not like me, she'll say. Loving someone who's in love with a rock in the sea is why, she'll say, someday Liam will leave.

She describes her travels, her life *upstream*, she always says, and that Winter Island is just not practical for anyone with an *itch*. She describes her life like this itch—she must go where the wind takes her. That her life was too big for her, that this place, and my father, and, I guess, me too, weren't enough to make her stay. She does all of our talking.

"There was a little bookshop in Chelsea that let us sell our fresh macaroons," she said.

But she meant: *You should have everything you want,* and *Liam will just get in the way.*

"Before you lived in this little house, your father and I used to sneak onto this land and kiss for hours," she says.

My mother liked to revisit these kinds of stories, the ones where she really loved him, and when this island felt like her biggest adventure. She describes the twisted vines near the pond, the always-full moons, the frogs at night. She says the island people are always looking for a way home. Says she can remember her own footprints on top of the wet sand at the lowest tide. She knows the smell of the black forest on the dark end of this island, overrun with rabid animals, and she mentions the tide pools that are full of things that can breathe underwater. She knows the best climbing trees. The views. The places to fall in love.

I pull this month's tide chart from my back pocket, and we examine it together, her head leaning close to mine, and from behind, we must be the same sloping shoulders. I decide it's too late and the tide is too high to visit the tide pools, and she says something like, *Oh, you really do know everything about this place.* I can't tell her that I know this island better than she does. I flip the pages of the little book and trace my finger along the wavelength lines of numbers, and it's the perfect time for her to ask me about my research and my teaching and what I've done at the Sea Institute. But she's never taken my career seriously; she says teaching college kids about the ocean is a waste of time, because there are no real answers and no one really knows what's lurking beneath.

"There will be a perfect low tide for the wedding," I say.

"You think it's a bad sign?" she asks.

"Lots of room on the sand for tables," I say.

"You're getting everything you want," she says.

It's hard to look her in the eye. We stare at the flames.

"You can say anything to me—you're my daughter," she says.

I find some courage, and the beer is working. It all comes out so fast, and I regret it as soon as it seeps out. It's like poison.

"Why are you here?" I ask.

"Can't a mother come to her daughter's wedding?"

"I guess."

"You don't want me here," she says.

"You hate it here," I say.

THERE WERE MANY times when my mother came back. She'd complain about the ferry as she swooped me up for a day of adventure. It happened at least once a year, never on a birthday or holiday, but she'd suddenly appear and ask me about school, or boyfriends, or weed, or whatever. She offered her versions of wisdom, comfort, womanhood. On one of these trips, she brought me my first black bra from the mainland, and she told me how to shave my pussy: *But not too much pressure, because those razor bumps will sting in salt water, and when you have sex, your bumps will feel like they are on fire.*

Another time, she took me to Los Angeles for a stamp collectors' show and then she asked me, over ice cream, in the Great Western Forum, if I was really happy on Winter Island. Before I could even answer, she gawked at cases of vintage postage stamps and was negotiating her way to a collector's Elvis sheet. She outbid four others. What I found: my mother wasn't crazy; she just didn't want me as much as I wanted her. My father said she simply had too much to give to the rest of the world.

We burdened ourselves with excursions full of busy-work, she talked and I did the listening. We'd swim, visit the zoo, shop, run errands, plant flowers, clean tables at restaurants—anything to keep our hands busy and our thoughts quiet. Our meditative state had become something we did so well together—all the not saying of things—and it'd become a ritual for her to ask questions without wanting any answers.

SHE IS PACING around my kitchen now with her mouth full of my bread, and there's yellow oil dripping from her chin. Like she's sucked out the insides of something once living. We've agreed in our silence to forgive again, and I change the subject.

"I've got to pick up my dress tomorrow," I say.

"Is it white?" she asks.

I'm nodding, chewing.

"Is that little Korean woman still at the tailor shop?" she asks.

I'm face-full nodding.

There's a cool draft creeping through the ancient windows, and it's this time of night when the winds change and everything blows onshore. The nighttime sea breeze rushes into my house, and then the dogs always know it's dinnertime. Tonight, though, the whale stink is dreadful, and it's like we're sitting in a puddle of funk. The dogs rustle into the kitchen, their nails scratching against the wood floors. I give them leftover chicken, and as their tags clink against their metal bowls, my mother and I make our way back to the fire, to avoid the smell and all the other things. The dogs eat quickly, plagued by the rancid stench, and then they run into the back room to hide. Like it's earthquake weather, like they know that something is coming.

"That whale just might ruin this whole thing," she says.

"There are ways to get rid of whales."

"Can't one of your sea friends blow it to pieces?" she asks.

"We'd have sharks forever," I say.

"Kill them, too," she says.

"They'd just come back," I say.

I toss her blankets and pillows from the cedar chest that I keep next to the couch. Then I squeeze her hand.

I say, "You're going to help me drag that whale out to sea."

Tsunami

We lied about many things, but we never lied about weather. The constant foreboding of eerily colored skies, the dry summer winds, and the densely fogged harbor mornings did not hide. Even the mainlanders saw weather hovering over Winter Island as if it were a wall of dry island that had erupted from the Pacific Ocean to protect Los Angeles from oncoming absurdities. It sprouted from the bottom of the sea, angry and no stranger to loneliness.

That day, we thought the tsunami was just a hoax. A seaman rang the bell as he rounded the harbor. Preparations were made. Windows boarded. Evacuations planned. A deep chill lingered, and Dad had to hide his weed and coke. Just in case, he said. Just in case we made it out alive, he meant.

We were renting a room in back, the only way we could live like that, from two baseball players who were Dodgers, or once-Dodgers, and who had invested their injury retirement money into a monstrous vacation home on the Western Shore of Winter Island. In the early mornings, the neatly packed mansions left a shadow upon the sea. My whole world was a pile of sparkly jewels, salty men who loved the bottle, and rich families who vacationed for sport.

I don't know how Dad met the twins—maybe through cocaine slanging, or jokes over beers, or friends of friends—but Dad loved living in that glass-walled-concrete monstrosity. It had a pool.

Dad raised me like a boy, and with mostly no mother and many cardboard boxes of macaroni-and-cheese dinners. Sometimes we'd have hot dogs with fancy German names, and sometimes we'd eat a box of warm doughnuts with small cartons of chocolate milk. Sometimes we had money; sometimes we didn't. Sometimes there were storms, and sometimes sunburns. We lived on fake money, famous money, and drug money, and always, it was just enough to never leave the island.

It was my fifth-grade teacher who parted metal blinds and gulped at the darkness building over the Pacific and said it was coming. That we'd all have to go home quickly. Without lunch. I scrounged nickels from other people's desks for a bag of Doritos and walked the shoreline home. The sea smelled saltier, and the air, thicker, and I shoved chips in my mouth, in case that was dinner.

Dad heard it on the TV while he was railing lines with the twins in the kitchen. They said it was coming and nothing could stop it. We were all to leave Winter Island. Los Angeles sent its gratitude to the little island that protects it from the wrath of the ocean, the newswoman said.

"You're fucking welcome," Dad said to the TV.

Islanders started a steady evacuation, and then dark pillows of clouds came. Neighbors sandbagged their doors and taped up windows. Otto House pedaled its hotel guests to the ferry on surrey bikes, with luggage tied to the sagging canvas top. Dad and the twins moved the bikes and pool toys into the garage. The ferry would close by twilight, and then we'd be on our own.

"We're not fucking leaving," he said.

"Will it really wash us away?" I asked.

Dad, who was born on Winter Island, said we'd stay, that we'd have a party to celebrate that monumental blessing from Mother Nature. No matter what could happen, he was not going to leave. He said we'd be just fine, like always, and that if the ship were *motherfucking going down*, we were going, too.

We bought the last of the ground beef from the butcher, and enough other food for a few days. Just in case the island actually flooded and the ferries never came back, Dad said we'd need protein, and that he could cook anything by fire.

Dad said we'd be okay until help came or, as the twins suggested, we'd be better yet if no one ever came back. We bought the last of the old Easter candy on the sale aisle, water balloons just in case there would be time for fun, all of the chips, and a bag of apples, because the twins liked to eat healthy. When we returned home, I broke into the chips like they were a cherished birthday present and ate them without caution. Perhaps we should have planned our rations better. Perhaps we should have considered leaving then, so we wouldn't be stuck there forever. Alone.

THE OXYCONTIN PILL guy and Dad's coke friend stopped in. They were preparing for the end of the world, with the amount of illegal treasures they stashed in our kitchen drawers.

"You want cheese on your burger?" Dad asked.

He was wearing his KISS THE KOOK apron.

"Let's eat before this rain gets too heavy," he said.

Those who weren't leaving—the other single dads, a few Playmates the twins had over often, and the other beach druggies—began to take shelter at our place. They jumped in the pool and screamed things about the end of days.

By late afternoon, I could feel something was different. The color left. The clouds crept closer until they hung overhead. Dad and his buddies were so high they didn't notice. I floated on a plastic raft and watched black clouds cover the sun, smashing potato chips into my mouth and slowly swaying to the sound of waves nearby. Light rain tickled my face and made tiny pops against the pink plastic inflatable. I called for Dad, but the music was too loud. It all reminded me of the last eclipse—the time we stayed out all night to watch the moon turn into a purple sore and then watched *The Twilight Zone* on our little TV until there was sun.

The fake-boobied Playmates wore string bikinis before the real rain came. They draped the twins' press-conference-suit jackets over their shoulders and dipped their feet in the pool. They brought a gallon of Neapolitan ice cream and begged to braid my hair. I liked their tight gold skin and their painted-on eyebrows. They were like Barbies but bigger. The women that came in and out of that place were pretty and tall, and probably so nice to me because they pitied us. One of them would always feel so bad for Dad, so single and abandoned by a wretched, unloving woman. Those nights, I slept in my bunk alone.

The police were making their final rounds as the sun began to set. They begged people to leave. The lifeguards patrolled the dense, wet sand and boarded up their towers. They said there was no protection anymore. An officer had a clear plastic poncho stretched over his uniform. He commented on the chocolate dried to my face while he stood under the soaked porch awning—a place he often stopped to be part of the party when he could.

"You guys are on your own," he said.

The pill guy climbed to the roof, shirt off, and shouted at the sea. A dried nosebleed began to wash away from his face. He said that he could actually see the water receding. The news had said it would happen like that: We'd hit an all-time low tide, then an all-time high. There would be so much rising water that we'd flood and go under. If it hit us head-on, we might never see the mainland again. It wouldn't be a big wave, but a slow parade of water. The cokeheads cheered in anticipation while Dad wrapped me in a towel.

"Wash the chlorine out of your hair," he said.

We tossed water balloons in the rain, and the wild ones hollered at the clouds. At low tide, Dad bundled me in trash bags and a baseball cap and we followed his buddies to the shore. We stood like a wall, my hands protected by Dad's, and the pretty Playmates guarded the house behind us. The wind seeped through every crevice of our trash-bag clothes, and we whistled and whined at the extreme darkness spread evenly across the horizon. Together, we walked to where the sea met our feet. Mounds of dead sand crabs looked as if they'd died trying to find water, and the shrunken trash, broken shells, and seaweed were no longer a mysterious part of the ocean's floor.

"The pier is swaying," a twin said.

The lights were out at Rocky's Fish N Chips, and the rest of the old wooden pier stood like a bridge that had lost its way to land. Dad threw a piece of slimy seaweed at me. The twins found a wet tennis ball and traced the lines of a base-ball diamond in the sand with their toes while the rowdy wind whipped around and we sounded like sails in a storm. The pill guy swung a big stick at the ball, and as he rounded the trash-pile bases, Dad tagged him out. The sea slowly devoured our playing field, and with absolutely frozen toes, we hurried back to the house. Then, hard rain.

"Take a good look, Evie. It might be your last," OxyContin said.

Dad flicked him on the back.

"I'd never let anything happen to you," Dad said.

He always said it.

I ate the rest of the chips for dessert that night. Dad danced to records and spun me around in the office chair until I felt sick. Playmate Sasha taught me how to do the twist while rain pounded into the pool and a demonic wind rattled the windows.

Once we lost power, we crouched around lighted bath-room candles, and Sasha sang old country songs. The kind that made Dad's heart hurt. Then I was tucked in tightly on the top bunk for safekeeping.

We didn't hear all the water rising around us, or the sound of glass breaking, or the pool overflowing. We didn't hear nearby windows shatter or smell salt leaking into our living room. Dad was passed out cold, and I, dreadfully exhausted from chips and anticipation, slept though the worst of it.

In the morning, among the shadows made from partial sunshine, our house was flooded and smelled like a sunken ship. We had to paddle out in inner tubes and pool noodles to get anywhere on the bottom floor. Dad said not to swallow any of it. And when we recovered, red-eyed and lost, we began to clean up the mess. A cleanup that would take the actual rest of our lives. Still, we shouted wildly at the sea and called ourselves survivors.

Fog

For every funeral, I hoped my mother would return to me, wearing her jewelry and curled hair, and for every dead body, I'd send for her by letter to a hopeful address, only to have the letter returned. Even if just for one afternoon, I needed her. I never said it to Dad, but I know he wanted her back, too, because he shaved close to his face and wore cologne. He said it was to honor the dead, but I knew it was for my mother. When Old Tropez died, I secretly believed my mother would appear, in beautiful shell necklaces and turquoise earrings, sprinkling white petals on his grave. I waited.

Dad and I collected unscathed shells and beach glass, carefully in silver pails. We walked along the windy stretch of the Western Shore, and the rich people had left their mansions and gone back to the mainland for the winter. Those hours were spent in silence. My arms were tired from the gathering, and I told my father I ached. The buckets were heavy the whole way home. Dad drilled holes into the shells, and while he sat in silence by the fire, I strung the pieces onto long strands of twine, complaining that my back and hands hurt, wanting to ask why we decorated coffins with shells. Soon, there were endless ringlets of glittering shells that glowed in the almost-darkness. Tropez was still dead. Still no mother.

"Was it a heart attack?" I asked.

"I think so," Dad said.

But I really wanted to know the *how*, what it looked like when someone leaves forever.

"Better sleep—you'll need your strength for tomorrow," he said.

I was always the only girl to carry the casket.

"Did you get a good look at him?" I asked.

"These aren't questions for little girls."

But he told me the answers anyway, because whether we said it aloud or not, I was never a little girl. He said the old man dropped right at his feet, slammed his face against the dock, and, without me asking, Dad told me what I wanted to know: that his eyes were closed, and that sometimes, loneliness can make a heart stop.

ONCE, MY MOTHER told me about the Mariana Trench. The deepest part of the sea, and the darkest. I knew about darkness before she spoke of the trench, but no book or visit to the Sea Institute had revealed just how deep and dark this trench was. The morning she told me, straight from her memory, I pretended to be a whale on the living room floor. I slithered and kicked my feet like they were a tail, and I made sounds of echolocation. She was in the kitchen, and there was coffee and toast.

Sometimes she'd call me for breakfast in her own whale voice, which was shrill and terrifying, and I loved it. She used to open every window in that apartment, the one with the wraparound deck, and she'd prop me up on a chair and tell me to search for whale spouts. Some mornings, my mother read out loud about the Mariana Trench: *More than one thousand times the standard atmospheric pressure at sea level.* I repeated it back to her.

THE MORNING WE were to bury Old Tropez's body, my father swam in the sea. I could see his arms rhythmically digging in and out of the ocean for hours. A thick layer of fog coated everything. When he made his way back, he said, *Salt cures everything.* He made eggs. I listened for the door. He shaved close. His cologne. He said the fog brought death. Or the death brought the fog. Or it was just neither, or both. He said that I was twelve, and I should know about the dying things, and what they mean.

"I want to be buried at sea," I blurted out.

"It's too dark, and too big, and how will you know how to get back here?" he asked.

Other days, we walked through the cemetery on top of the hill. We sat by his mother's grave, or we traipsed around the damp lawn to stretch our legs and he'd point out where he wanted to sleep forever.

Once, he pulled me close, our sides smashed together, and I could feel his bony shoulder pressed against my temple. Always: the smell of fish, salt, beer, and stale pretzels. He pointed to a grassy hill that bloomed with wildfire color after the rains. That was the place. I couldn't help but think of all the times we had been lost, and how it might be easier without him if I really wanted to find the way.

ATOP THE FOGGY, wild bluff, a captain read poetry to the men huddled around the coffin. We laid flowers and trailed shells on top, and Dad spoke, too. For the first time since my mother left, I saw him cry, and it must have been for a million things. He laid a piece of white sailcloth on top of the wood, and when he backed away, he looked like a child.

I looked around for my mother. Only walls of gray.

When the fog began to clear, there were traces of blue sky. Everyone talked quietly, and then men drank from the bottles they kept in their jacket pockets.

"You're quiet," Dad said.

I was really thinking of ways to leave my father. Passages to find my mother. I was daydreaming of Jason W from homeroom. The way his sweatshirt was always too big, and how it bounced every time he made a layup. I was tired, in fact, from staying up all night and forcing myself to think only of Jason W, just so I didn't have to think about everything else. I was tired of feeling alone, even when my father was sleeping on the couch outside my bedroom door. I was tired.

"Just sad," I said.

ONCE, MY MOTHER talked about atmospheric pressure. Said there was pressure all over, even in the deepest, darkest trench. My mother didn't like this pressure, said it felt like she might explode. She closed the windows and used wooden dowels to lock them shut. I said something like, *There's so much pressure that your heart can explode.*

When she went away, I learned this pressure, the weight inside my chest. There was the pressure of missing things, the leaving of things, the invisible weight that felt so thick, even when everything was still moving. She taught me the constant foreboding of implosion.

THE FUNERAL PROCESSION led the men to the bar, and Dad told me to walk faster. They drank. I read in my nook behind the bar, where I had learned to hide so as to let the drunken buzz of their voices lull me to sleep. Where I could imagine my life with Jason W—the kind of life where we'd have a boat in every size, and islands to match their splendor. I tried to think of Jason W's bony knees and flashing green eyes. I replayed his hands dribbling a ball, to block out the grievers' drunk wails. I tried to read. I read the same paragraph over and over. I pictured Jason W grabbing me by the hand and leading me past my father, to the parking lot, into a car, onto the ferry, over to the mainland, how we'd promise never to stop moving. His baggy sweatshirt.

I drank last sips of beer from the drunken bereaved. My first real buzz. Women came with flowers. Dad stood on top of the bar for some drunken speech. Jason W's mother brought lasagna.

Then, I heard him dribbling the ball outside the back door.

"I thought you were in there," Jason W said when I emerged from the bar.

The ball bouncing echoed against the alley walls.

"Sad day," I said.

"My parents bought his fish," he said.

I never told my father about Jason W's parents inviting me over to dinner so often. Or that we met in detention, because I was so often late. Or that Jason W got detention for bad things, like stealing. That he was known for giving hickeys in the woods of Ferry Lands. From the window, I saw my father slurp a forkful of lasagna right from the pan, and there was cheese stuck to his blotched, drunken face.

"You want to sneak onto Ferry Lands?" he asked.

"No."

"Tin Pan Carnival?" he asked.

"K."

But I knew it was closed for the season. We walked until I needed his sweater, and until we reached the empty Ferris wheel with an empty booth that we slouched in for a few hours. He talked about basketball and I talked about whale books, and we didn't say all the things about darkness. Eventually, we decided that Jason W should be my first boyfriend and, eventually, one day, slip his fingers down my pants. He proved his devotion with one solid, quiet kiss, our lips cold. We were far away from my father. And mother. And still, there was a world out there.

MY MOTHER SAID orcas have the same eyes as humans, that if you look deep enough they seem endless. I asked her if she believed there were undiscovered things in the sea, and she said there were undiscovered things everywhere. She asked me to imagine the pit of the Mariana Trench, that place where even humans couldn't reach, the center of the Earth, the darkness. The fish there have headlights, she said. There will be plenty of things I won't understand, she said. But there must be paths to those places unknown, she said. Told me to keep searching. Searching in complete darkness.

Killer Whale

Orcinus orca

QUESTION: Why do orca pods (both aggressive and non-aggressive) hunt marine mammals by working together?

Because your father is charming, he will not say if he owns the boat. He will let you call him Captain, even when he's only a deckhand, or a drug buddy of the boat's owner. He will lead your entire sixth-grade class, and teacher, and teacher's assistant, to believe that he owns the boat and the captain's hat, and that he is a master seaman. He will say that despite their name, killer whales are social and they work together to get what they want. To hunt other mammals.

No one will say anything about the booze he is drinking out of a coffee cup, though the adults must know it's booze. Instead, you will allow everyone to believe that your father is the type of father who owns a boat and a captain's hat, one who has sailed the world ten times over. That would explain his tan. His worldly views. His reason for settling on this magnificent island, because, as he says, his ancestors were founders.

When the boat creeps out of a misty harbor, past a buoy of lazy sea lions, and picks up speed on top of all that open water, you won't tell him to turn back. You won't tell him to slow down. Though you know he's going the wrong way, and that he's going too fast, and that he's talking to the class as if he is of scientist blood. You'll believe he knows everything, too. This is why you'll spend your life seeking so many answers.

In the winter, there will be orcas off the coast of Winter Island, he'll say.

Will we see them today, Captain? a student will shout.

Your father will promise orcas, bottlenose dolphins, common dolphins, rays, clear water, and at least one fluke that will smash against the sea and splash your friends. He'll say the whales know *his* boat. And as the boat moves faster, the horizon will become tangled with the sun shining in your eyes, and because of your father's charm and his ability to just often enough keep his promises, there will be dolphins and whales. They'll breach out of the water and slam so hard back into the sea. You'll want to cheer, but your stomach will be sick. The rest of your class will clap and snap photos, and even your lady teachers will now be very interested in calling him Captain.

You're the only one who will puke. You'll hide in the cabin below, because you've been on this boat many times: for retirement soirees, for funerals, for weekend tiki-themed drug parties with Playmates and baseball players. Once there was Mick Jagger, although your father made you stay in the tiny cabin below for that party. You've always liked that boat, because you could get a lot of reading done when it was just circling, slowly, around Tin Pan Harbor. You've never felt the horror of open water until your father promises to show your sixth-grade class a pod of whales.

He'll find you below—who fucking knows who is behind the wheel—and he'll wipe your forehead with a cool rag. He'll make a joke that you can't be his daughter because you can't live at sea, and you can't really be related to him if you *don't got sea legs*. He'll say you are either born with these legs or you are not. You'll hear the whales blowing air and the children screaming at the mist evaporating into the sky.

If you sit down here, it will make it worse, he'll say. *Look at the straight line of the horizon.*

You'll manage to climb up the twisted stairs to the bow, and you'll lean over and throw up what feels like every single meal you've ever eaten in your life. Your dad will tell stories about the sea, and everyone will watch the horizon with wide eyes. You'll think that now, while you are still dumping your insides into the Pacific, your teachers are drinking booze, too. You'll think you hear the clink of their porcelain mugs.

He'll pick up speed again; he knows how to drive the boat. Against the restless moving of the sea, you'll be going so fast that the boat is smashing against whitecapped waves. You'll have vomit on your windbreaker. You'll keep throwing up as everything goes faster. Then there will be sea lions, and common dolphins, racing along the hull, and you'll rest your head on your arms, which you glue to the side of the boat. You'll miss the sea by a few feet by the time you are throwing up bile, and it's everywhere.

Other children will crowd around you, some will run away at the sight and smell of you, and finally a teacher with beer breath brings you a towel. She'll say she's surprised it's you, and that no one else got seasick; she's also so surprised that your father is wonderful. Not the first time you have heard this. Not the first time he drove too fast and forgot that you were suffering alongside him.

Your father will insist that he'll take your picture hanging over the bow of the boat with a disposable camera. As torture. As a memory. As a reminder that his charm will find you a pod of whales, or dolphins, or anything else that you're looking for.

Rain

Everything was wet; our bathroom towels never dried, and pieces of my hair became a stranger's ringlets. We had things shipped from the mainland because there wasn't enough on the island to keep anyone dry: rain boots, tarps, ropes, umbrellas. We made ferry runs so often to get supplies. We'd return damp. Our bones must have been made of water.

Underneath the great statue of Francis of Paola lie the vast, fertile fields of grasses and the grove of citrus trees of Ferry Lands. Now abnormally green from the rains and the floods, it is a massive patch of land that stretches across the most crucial part of the island. Francis stands on a slab of granite that is the mouth of the harbor, where he is watchful of seamen who pass through our waters. He blesses the lost with one hand on his heart, and with the other, points to the wavering horizon. His closed eyes are made of shells, and his body built of rock that has survived all weather. Except his fingers have chipped, and sometimes we find shells to put him back together.

Mary was the groundskeeper of Ferry Lands, and possibly the only other woman my father loved as much as my mother. We stayed so many nights in her small bungalow near the lighthouse, my father telling jokes, and Mary making everything warm. During the rainy season, Mary spent her days packing sandbags. She lived by candlelight and foghorns, and concerned herself with the illumination of the lighthouse onto the nighttime sea. She listened. She traced the same lines back and forth from the mainland to Tin Pan Harbor each day as she drove the ferry for a little bit of money and that small, watchful house. Dad convinced her to let the Sea Institute run an oceanography summer camp, for kids to explore the tide pools. Nearly every child on the island enrolled that year. Some were shuttled from the mainland, and the swarm of yellow buses left tire marks on her soggy lawns. Later, Dad helped her lay gravel for a new driveway.

Sometimes, my father and Mary hiked up to the statue and ate a picnic dinner upon the oversized feet. They'd come back smelling like weed and wine. Sometimes, I went, too, and Dad told origin stories of California and the Channel Islands. Sometimes, we waited for great migrations of whales. On a blanket, we laughed together and let our food settle while we lay on our backs waiting for rain. And when it came, we ran down the hills, through the acres of pristine land, past the citrus trees and muddy ponds, to Mary's home, which after a while felt like ours, too.

There was always ice cream. Mary and Dad danced to Fleetwood Mac in a living room made of tiny seashelled walls. Dad and I bunked on separate couches that faced each other, with our feet closest to the fire, and when I was pretending to be asleep, he'd sneak down the creaky hallway to be with Mary. Eventually, I slept so soundly.

"Maybe this is our home," I said.

Dad squeezed my hand.

He said he'd never met a woman like her—not with wild gray hair and masculine hands and sun freckles and a strong back. He'd never met a woman who was healthy and sad, and happy and warm, too. He said she was unlike the others. Compared to his other women, her breasts were swollen in the wrong places and they hung low. She knew of all the living things in the warm waters and all the things lurking in the dark ones. She told stories of the moon, of the land, of the people who came to own this island when *it sprouted up like a wild spring flower begging for sun.* And she loved me.

But it was like my mother could smell our happiness from afar. When she came looking for us, we were sitting on Mary's porch sipping coffee—mine decaf in a tin cup— and we must have looked like a family: Dad's hand was on

Mary's knee while she read the paper's travel section aloud. I examined migration charts and pretended to know the way of the whales by drawing lines with pencils on sprawled-out maps. The quietest we ever were.

"I've looked everywhere for you," my mother said.

Dad stood and met her at the bottom of the steps, so as not to let her cross the threshold of contentedness, and she slipped slightly into the ground when her wedged shoe dug into the wet gravel.

"The house looks great," she said.

"Took Evie and me a few good coats," Dad said.

"You got running water here, Mary?" she shouted.

Mary smiled, kept reading the paper, and didn't look up when she said, *Of course, dear.*

My mother said she'd been released from a three-month appointment in the Galápagos, where she'd been studying dying marine life, specifically, she said, the turtles. She pulled a hand-carved wooden turtle from her purse and dangled it in the light. She said she thought the turtles were coming back, that maybe the ocean wasn't warming as fast as they'd once believed.

"Evie, do you still like sea turtles?" she asked.

But it was whales—it had always been whales—and it was Mary who spent hours telling me of the great migrations now, even if she didn't tell me in her own whale voice.

I hung my hand out over the porch railing and took my mother's turtle.

"A woman in town makes all kinds of carvings out of wood," she said. "I'll take you there someday, and you can pick out anything you want."

The problem with the turtle: it was marvelously intricate and beautiful.

Then, Mary must have known that no matter what, I'd always love my mother more than I'd love her. Then, Mary knew my father was under the same spell. It was impossible to commit to Mary when we hadn't finished uncommitting to my mother. Sometimes, that desperate hope of her coming back, or her wanting us again, was all we had. Some days, especially when she stood right in front of us, like she'd really come back for us, it was impossible to fight our demon of hope. And even though Mary was what we needed, it was my mother who needed so badly to be wanted.

"You want some coffee?" Mary said to my mother.

"I was hoping to take Evie to see a movie."

Dad moved from the steps and let me pass. He said to be home before dark.

WHEN MY MOTHER would return out of nowhere she would take me to the aquarium on Winter Island. Only open for summer. Everything was periwinkle and cracking, and the tanks were moldy and muddled. Smelled like a wet shoe/ beard, and it really felt like living underwater. My mother would pretend to hold her breath, with puffed cheeks, and motion her arms like she was swimming, probably just to avoid the smell, and she shuffled her feet on the wet gray carpet. She'd let me press my face to the tank, and then she'd tell me to hold my breath. Our cheeks full of air. *Like this*, she'd say. My mother let me feed the seal a silvery fish. Each time, she'd buy me a jellyfish balloon animal, and by the time it deflated she was gone.

The aquarium closed every September. I would linger just for the smell. Blow up a balloon and spend hours making tentacles out of shells, string, glue, crepe paper, toilet paper, anything I could find to make a better, longer-lasting jelly-fish. Dad would wake to the sound of the balloon squeaking against my hands. I'd add two tiny marker dots for eyes, so she could peer out the window and watch for fall or for my mother, until the sun wilted her body, but I imagined that my mother would have told me she was beautiful.

WHEN I RETURNED to Dad and Mary, my cheeks were rosy. My mother and I had been sitting at the outside café at the mainland mall for hours before Mom emptied a dollop of sunscreen into my palm. By then, it was too late. I was burned. I was full on unlimited fries and Mom's secondhand smoke.

She dropped me at the bottom of the long driveway and said Dad probably didn't want to see her anyway. And her shoes wouldn't make that trek again. And she asked, *Is he in love with her?* and I kissed her on the cheek and trotted back to where the window was foggy and aglow. I traced the valleys and caverns on the wooden turtle's back with my thumb the whole way up the driveway.

Dad was drunk on the steps. He'd been crying. Even in the barely light and the moving dense fog, I could see right into him, the heap of hotness that had overcome him. His face was pink.

"We can't stay here anymore," he said.

Our things were neatly packed into paper shopping bags on the porch, and there were a few wool blankets that weren't even ours. Whiskey bottles. He said he'd come back for the books and the teakettle. And then he told me what he must have told Mary that same day: he had been given a boat, and there was space enough for only two people. Other things he must have said: *I can't do this anymore, because maybe I don't know love.* Or: *I am afraid of this love, and the last, and all the others that might come after.*

No one asked me if I wanted to live on a boat.

"Mary said you can come here anytime, Evie."

The walk to the harbor wasn't more than a few miles, but it felt like it took the entire night. When we stopped for Dad to take a few swigs, I looked for Mom's car—if that was even her car—and it was impossible to see. Maybe she'd stayed. The more he drank, the less he made sense of things, and the more he apologized.

"How did you get a boat?" I asked.

"It's for the best," he said.

The boat was a gift, or a donation, from one of the rich summer families on the Western Shore. He said it was because he had worked so hard in the off-season watering their lawn, trimming their bonsais, and feeding their pet snake. And maybe Dad had been privy to the affair the wife was having with the off-season Jacuzzi installer from the mainland. Dad wouldn't have told anyway, because he never gave a shit about that kind of pointless affair, but when she divided up the assets in the divorce, somehow my father got a boat.

"A pity boat?" I said.

"A free boat," he said.

The paper bags were weakened by dampness by the time we found our slip. He was too drunk to do anything but unlock the cabin door and pass out on the padded dining room bench. Instead of looking for a light, I fell asleep in a chair. Didn't unpack until morning, when Dad woke me to a cup of hot chocolate and a box of our books and trinkets. My wooden turtle was nestled on the ledge of the kitchen window that overlooked the harbor.

Dad boasted that we'd won our freedom, and I tried to make the best of our new home. He said I could have my own bunk and that I could put a KEEP OUT sign on the small sliding door. That we could get a bookshelf. That we could smell the glorious fresh fish hauls and the gull shit, and that we'd fall asleep to the sound of sea lions lingering loudly on a buoy. That sometimes, there were dolphins that had lost their way in the harbor, that were trapped for days, that jumped and squealed. But it wasn't Mary's house, and it wasn't her kitchen in the morning with coffee, and Dad laughing and laughing. The ground beneath was no ground at all; we were always sinking.

"This is our place forever, or until you marry rich and buy me a mansion," Dad said.

The first few months on the boat were spent reading, bathing in the vanishing sunshine, sleeping to the sound of rain falling on top of water, eating all the freshest seafood and Chinese takeout. But I missed my mother, and even more, I wondered how she'd ever find us on a boat. I missed Mary more. Dad drank less. He smoked more weed. He did push-ups on the bow. He put fresh flowers in a pitcher and left them on the table. I wasn't sure if they were for me, or my mother, or Mary.

Every minute felt like we were just trying to keep busy, like we were missing something, and though we always blamed this feeling on my fleeting mother, it was really the new life we'd built at Ferry Lands that was missing. Maybe for once, we'd discovered what it meant to be a family, and it scared my father so much that he turned his back.

I loved my father so much then, without anyone else to make it better or worse—just him, and his jokes and his marinated steaks. There were hours of Uno and backgammon, and the fish were plentiful, and there was some money, too. Still, I needed Mary.

It took months for her to come see our boat. Even more time for her to forgive my father for not committing to her and us, but eventually she arrived on our dock with provisions to keep us fed and warm. Her hair was longer and wirier, but she wore the same fleece sweater, and she pointed to the edge of our small ship. EVANGELINE THE SECOND, painted in blue. There were flowers on our kitchen table again.

I did all the talking at first, doing them both a favor, and I showed Mary my reading nook and my mother's jewelry box perched in a built-in compartment in my bunk. We talked about a seal that was obnoxiously loud in the mornings—*like a fucking rooster*, Dad said—and she said the state of California was considering building a bridge to the mainland. We ate teriyaki chicken in the small booth on the stern, and I refilled Mary's cup with iced tea we'd brewed in the last of the late-summer sun.

I said I had homework when I left them. I pressed my ear to my porthole to try to listen to every word they said.

At first, Mary said she understood. He could only love her so much. Dad liked to revel in his own damage, though, and started to sound like a fool. Evie comes first, he said. Then, it seemed like my mother was in the way, and that he couldn't pass up the boat. He said it was his only chance to finally make it on his own, and maybe that was more important that making it with anyone else. She left shortly after a long wave of silence, during which I imagined they were kissing or he was holding her, and when my father returned inside, I pretended to read a book.

"You okay?" he asked.

"You okay?" I asked.

SOMEHOW, THEY'D FOUND some closure between them, and I managed to conceal a smile if I saw her at the butcher shop or the post office. Sometimes I'd miss her so much that I let Jason W give me hickeys in the thick trees of Ferry Lands, true to his reputation, hoping she'd catch me and yell at me and call my father, and we'd be invited to a real dinner in her kitchen. But for a while, we tried to unlearn the longing, until there were sirens warning of an incoming storm.

The August harbor was abandoned by most who tried to avoid the downpour. The winds kicked around hail, and little pieces of ice fired from the sky. The Coast Guard cruised through the harbor and barked over a loudspeaker that due to the impending high tide, severe wind, and rainstorm, we should evacuate. But on that day, there wasn't anywhere to go. We'd exhausted all possible stays, Dad didn't have any drug buddies left on the mainland who weren't in jail, and, worse, he believed he was stronger than any storm.

"I won't let anything happen to us," Dad said.

The boat thrashed and thrust its hull against the dock as we scurried to secure buoys and stuff away trinkets and outdoor furniture. The water rose and covered the barnacles on the seawalls. We played cards inside, and Dad drank until he was drunk enough to give me a swig of whiskey. He said we would ride it out.

Night fell quickly, with dark clouds crowding in early, and eventually, it felt like we were forever on high seas. I was so nauseated when we started to take on water, when the patio chairs were floating freely in the harbor, when the wind bashed up the thick body of the boat. In the blanket of windy rain, we had to abandon ship.

I shoved my wooden turtle in my pocket and a few books down my pants as we escaped. Our hands were full of whatever we could carry, and we scurried 2.1 miles up that messy road to Ferry Lands.

Wordlessly, Mary opened the door and made us dry by the fire. With only the sound of pounding rain on her roof, she left us blankets and disappeared down the darkness of the hall.

In the morning, she left us hot coffee and her refolded newspaper, and there was a note for Dad. He never revealed the contents. We left at the first sign of midmorning light.

Evangeline the Second sank to the bottom of the sea, and we knew we'd never be able to pay to get her out. For a day, Dad let us be devastated that our last hope for a real life had been submerged by the Pacific and lurking like an ancient city below. For the next few weeks, Dad passed out after dinner and we lugged around shopping bags from couch to couch. We spent hours staring at the sea.

"I'm sorry I can't give you anything," Dad said.

We sat on a bench, watching clumsy waves crash on top of each other, and leftover storm-cleanup crews plucking unwanted mainland trash that had washed up on the sand. He put his hand on mine and apologized again.

"You can't control the weather," I said.

Because what else do you say to a father you are fathering?

When we stopped talking about that storm, the one that washed out half of our harbor, we spent our afternoons at Rocky's Fish N Chips so Dad could drink frozen margaritas with salt, and charm his way back onto another fishing boat.

One day, a bartender handed us an envelope with Mary's perfect penmanship scrawled across its white face. It was a thick wad of cash. No note. It was enough to get us into an apartment again, and we knew better than to ask any questions. That night, we ate double cheeseburgers with extra cheese, and the next day we took our shopping bags and our books and our collected things to a cheap bungalow that had a one-bedroom alcove that I covered with a sun-moon-stars curtain, and there was a splendid view of the ocean.

The next summer, there was our boat, dug out from the bottom of the sea, restored into an entirely new being. It was freshly painted and named *Sound of a Woman That Loves You*.

Heat

My father had never wanted me to do the adult things he did on the island—drink too much, fuck, do drugs, sell drugs, grow weed, pass out in jail cells—until I started bleeding. It was so hot that I didn't know what was blood and what was sweat. My mother, and other women, had left remnants of tampons and pads, and Dad slipped them all under the slit of the door, one at a time. Two tampons and nine pads.

For July Fourth, mainlanders came down from their Los Angeles hills at a steady pace, leading up to the holiday weekend. Pickup trucks unloaded thousands of pristine beach cruisers that had lived a nice life year-round in a garage. Mounds of people—families, college kids, and plenty of old divorced moms—took shelter in the island's overpriced weekend rentals. The rest of us rented out rooms and guesthouses for tons of cash, just for the holiday. There was enough money made that weekend to survive the rest of the summer, if you did it right. It was worth it to clean up the vomit and shit, blood and broken toilets, just for that tiny heartbeat in our pockets. Dad always came home with bags of cash. Sometimes, it was enough.

That year, I demanded that I wear my first two-piece in public. Dad agreed only if I promised to stay by his side. We must have both worried I would bleed right through. I didn't tell him that the tampon hurt.

We set out on bikes, the only way to get around in that kind of crowd, and crawled past roadblocks. Local police were already in riot gear, and they waved to Dad, offering an extra nod, because his small daughter trailed behind, in no more than a white-and-pink bikini. Perhaps they'd all recognized my swimsuit from *Island Love*, the semiporno-graphic series for very-late-night paid TV. No one told me Missy and Sissy left their costumes at our house for play. Dad never had the courage to tell me that the swimsuit came from a soft-porn set.

The tourists didn't look like us, and they didn't act like us, either. They treated Winter Island like a mythical place where they were excused for littering, double-parking, loitering, and any other sin that they could find for their holiday. They stepped on sea urchins and anemones, trashed our shore, and engaged in public sex for one weekend a year.

Heat radiated from parking lots, and the roads were a mess, with bikes, bells, and swarms of people carrying booze. We surveyed slowly, and Dad made his presence known. It was the first time I understood his livelihood. His absolute charm was our survival.

WINTER ISLAND IS shaped like a fish—the open mouth is Tin Pan Harbor, and its very small tail is called Fish Tail—a tight woodsy end with a clump of abandoned research buildings known to locals as the Old Institute, because scientists left the facilities to form the new, fully funded, prestigious Sea Institute on the mainland after the Cold War. The empty classrooms and tanks remain. Between the long stretch of uninhabitable rocks and clusters of trees sit a few hidden neighborhoods. Dad and I lived there when Mom first left—when we really had no money and were trying to get on our feet. The old bald guy who worked for months as a fisherman out of Tin Pan Harbor grew up in the bunkers, too, back when they were painted bright white, with manicured lawns.

So we rode to a place in the woods nearly unknown to the rest of the islanders: that patch of trailers and abandoned bunkers where there were traces of basketball courts and a parking lot. You never went to the Old Institute unless you needed a fix, a cheap plumber, or an excuse to thank your lucky stars that you weren't like all those sun-beaten leftovers. Or like us once, unless you were taking shelter in the dilapidated buildings of once-historical promise.

Billowing gray clouds gathered. Dad suggested I put on a shirt. I couldn't argue, though I was still sticky with sweat, because I wasn't sure what kind of monsters lingered in the woods or what kind of drunk men would notice my boobs.

Dad's friends, crowded in front of the trailers, were all so wrinkled, as if they'd never had shelter, and they were frying fish on a tiny barbecue. A stout woman hung red, white, and blue paper banners from her trailer to the next.

They had a perfect view of the sea—a private beach, too—but they were subjected to stronger winds than the rest of us on Winter Island. They built large dunes out of trash to protect their homes from high tides. It was a nice enough place for something that had once been completely abandoned. There was the dried-up dolphin tank.

Someone made a joke about the money we'd make from holiday tourists, and Dad and his friends filled our bags full of marijuana. We called it Winter Wonderland. It was how Dad survived in the world. It was grown in our most desolate woods, tucked behind the Old Institute, brought up on the world's crispest sea breeze and fertilized, we always said, by magical creatures that existed only on our island. It would turn out to be Winter Island's most valuable export, and people came from far and wide to get it.

Dad told me to go for a swim while he finished up business. I wore my shirt over my bikini. But as I tried to figure out how to then dry myself under the looming clouds, Dad decided I would carry the weed.

"I won't let anything happen to you, ever," he said.

He unrolled my backpack and shoved it full of Winter Wonderland. There was nothing to do except to follow directions.

I put on dry shorts. A trailer lady let me borrow a dry shirt, to make sure I looked thirteen, not like a mangled version of a real woman, the kind who would have sex for fun, or the kind who would get caught up selling drugs. Strapped to my back was the weed that would pay for breakfast, lunch, and dinner for the next three months after we sold it all. I'd never seen so much cash or smelled so much marijuana. It smelled of skunky wet dog rolling around in the coolest of mud.

We crept along the bike path. Dad knew where to find people who begged for Winter Wonderland. He'd casually walk along the beach, like he was an old man digging for gold, and then he would sit down in pockets of eager people and introduce me as a speed-reader, which I was, and a spectacular high diver, which I was, too, and any other charming anecdote to get conversations with strangers going. Then, casually, as people began to hand wads of cash to Dad, I'd reach in my backpack for the little dime-sized bags we were selling.

Maybe it was a rush to be near all the mainlanders, and to be near Dad like that.

I told him the bag was getting lighter.

"They'll be here all weekend," Dad said.

The boardwalk was so crowded by late afternoon: half-naked women with red, white, and blue face paint and itty-bitty crop tops, college students from near and far wrestling with addiction and peekaboo-nipple dresses, locals enjoying smoked meats and their massive pools and patios, and the sailing elite drinking endless champagne on yachts moored in Tin Pan.

I followed behind Dad, diligently, watching the back of his bike tire, and swerving and braking at the massive crowd swarming on the path. They were just tourists—they didn't know it was bikes-only—and Dad shouted at each one of them, *Wrong way, motherfucker.* Dad rang his bike bell to weave around the mess. He pedaled slowly, in case a summer tourist recognized him as the weed guy.

Then I screamed. Dad screeched his tires to a halt. The guys on all-black bikes, the ones who came every holiday season, crept too close while passing and smashed my finger when the ends of our handlebars hit. The blood dripped onto my shirt, onto Dad's hands, and he jumped off his bike in anger.

"Go sit the fuck on that bench," he told me.

Dad threw his bike to the sand and violently ripped the oily chain off the hearty metal. He charged the guys on the black bikes, specifically the one with a smug tourist face—threatening him with the chain, wrapping it around his neck, and telling them to get the fuck off the island. Everything was slipping with all the heat.

Dad's locals were beating the entire group of bike guys within seconds. And within minutes, Winter Island Police had clubbed and pulled them apart. They were all whisked away in cop cars, and I sat on the bench, with a bleeding hand and a hot-pink flowered backpack half-full of weed.

I walked to the shore, now almost desolate, because everyone had retreated to house parties to avoid the chilly afternoon winds, and I dunked my bloody hand into the ocean. Then it was like a thousand jellyfish sucking the blood from my fingers. I shook my hand dry as I climbed on my bike, double-checking that my bag was zipped properly. Still all the weed. I kept going, slow like Dad, toward home, wheeling Dad's broken bike alongside me.

The sun sank slowly over Winter Island, and a group of teenage boys stopped me.

"You the girl with Wonderland?" he said.

"Who's asking?"

"I got ten bucks," one said.

"Twenty," I replied.

They whispered for a minute, and the ugliest one of the group produced a crisp twenty-dollar bill. I handed them a bag, like this was a chosen profession I had trained for at a top vocational school.

"You wanna smoke with us?" Ugly said.

"I'm making dinner for my dad," I said.

There was a breeze, and I stood frozen. Beneath my bloodied shirt and tattered bikini were my nipples, cold and poking through. The boys stared. Hard. I stared back. My stomach knotted. They saw me and I saw them, and I wrapped myself with a towel like a cape and I mounted my bike. My tampon hurt.

I pedaled home faster, eager to take off the borrowed shirt and the itchy-as-shit bikini, and unwrapped a leftover sandwich in front of the TV. I pulled the plug of the tampon and flushed. Then I put on baggy sweats and Dad's giant sweater. Even though I was hot. I felt safe with the extra weight. I sweated while I cleaned the house and washed the dishes, so that when Dad came home in the morning, he would be able to rest.

Humpback Whale

Megaptera novaeangliae

QUESTION: Why is it believed that, like humans, humpbacks can feel emotions?

You will spend your nights reading for truths in books about the sea while your father is at a bar telling drunk tales of schooners and sharks and the unrecognizable sounds of whales. Your head will ache and your eyes will squint while you search for the things that are real on these pages of overdue library books. You'll read fast. You'll wait for him to come home. You'll shut off the light when you hear the door. You'll dream of the mean things in the ocean, even though they never touch you.

When your father finds your hoards of books, he will want you to return them before you've found any real answers. He'll say he can't afford any more late fees. So he'll share sweet kisses with Liz, the middle-aged librarian with a cane who he'd never really love, just so that you can keep all the late books you want. So that you can get *your answers*, he'll say.

When he's drunk, he'll read sections aloud, and he'll tell you that you've chosen all the wrong books. He will select a new stack for you to read, his version of an education, and place books next to your bedroom door. He'll ask you, *Did you find what you are looking for?*

He will quiz you about everything, and after reading enough, you'll know that it's possible that humans were whales and whales were humans, or something close to that idea. He will ask if you've ever been in love, to which you'll reply: *How should I know?*

Your father knows nothing of love, but he'll always say how much he loves you. Your father can love you and also love the tiny pebbles that roll onto the shore and cling to cold feet. There's no telling where all his love goes. Sometimes, you'll spend hours in encyclopedias asking: *Can love evaporate?* Once, you'll accidentally say it aloud, and Liz will tap you on the shoulder to tell you to keep it down.

He will take a few weeks to explain grunion—the silver fish that run to the sea beneath a full moon. He'll make you read the passages aloud. Until the words make a poem. He will wake you up in the middle of some night when there are sounds of whales breaching outside your window. He'll rush you like he's running from a tragedy, and you'll make it to the beach, where you sit in the darkness on the coldest sand, wrapped in the same blanket, half-asleep and watching the grunion migrate away from you and him. So fast it's as if the moonlit fish have legs. There will be light rain—he's packed a poncho for you—and he'll lure you closer to the sea. All of these field trips will be made in total silence, as if to hear the answers, and sometimes, after you find yourself home, with shelter, you'll still be quiet and forget to talk about the glowing eyeballs that just flooded the shore.

In the mornings, he will want answers. *What about whales*, he'll say. *Can they feel?*

You are just a daughter who wants to love him. But your life is all those lessons of his in nature: of calm and rough seas, of so many cryptic sea monsters, of things that live inside the Pacific. Some days, the metaphors are too messy and washed-out, and you'll just want to be loved back. Like, with a hug. He won't be the father you wanted, and he'll never find the mother you need, but still, he's yours and you are his, and you will have to navigate this together.

When your father holds court on the sand, in front of strangers, he'll tell tall tales of winds and eruptions, and things that sound like a dream. Even as you grow, even as your heart evolves like the spindle cells of the humpback whales that have been evolving for years, you will wonder which things are true. The love, or the stories, or none, or both.

Your research is ongoing.

Snow

Rook was the opposite of me: blond hair, wild blue eyes, and a rich father. She ran around Otto House in skimpy shorts and a flat chest puffed up to the sky. She told everyone in the lobby, or at school, or on the beach, that her father was the famous Los Angeles architect who designed Otto House in the 1970s. She said he was so inspired by the mystery and beauty of Winter Island that he decided to live there full-time, with Rook and his new plastic wife. Her real mother had died, and though mine hadn't, sometimes it felt the same. Their home on the Western Shore was featured in magazines from the mainland.

Rook hated to be disciplined, and she had a loud, dirty mouth. The only person who'd ever told her to shut up was Dad. And once, when we were kids at the Sea Institute oceanography summer camp, a camp leader told her if she didn't *shut the fuck up*, she'd be *sorry*. But her father got that woman fired the next day, and she wasn't sorry.

Once, she tried to sleep with a camp counselor, but he'd only give her tongue. She was the youngest girl I knew to talk about sex, because she was full of sex, and by the time I was old enough to tell her about Jason W fingering me on the beach, she was already getting fucked by college-boy tourists. We started smoking cigarettes behind the hotel.

"I know your dad sells weed," she said.

"You say you know everything," I said.

People came to Winter Island for my father. He knew how to tell the story of a land of wild forests covered in fog and trolls and gnomes. He grew the best weed in the world. He made it worldwide-famous. He told tales of wild deer effortlessly bouncing through rows of lush greens tucked away among the dark canyons of our island.

During the day, and for extra cash, my father drove tour groups in unmarked vans to the top of our dormant volcano, where each year, with the light dusting of mountaintop snow, he'd decorate a small tree with shells and lights. He worked part-time at Otto House as a concierge, as a quiet drug dealer, as a heart-of-gold dad who needed free rooms every once in a while because he often had nowhere else to stay. He diligently kept a notebook of guest nicknames, favorite drugs, restaurants, and beachside activities, because he believed in the value of customer service.

Did Rook know all that?

My run-ins with Rook as a child were limited; I had only heard rumors about her on playgrounds and, as we got older, from other jealous-type girls who said she stuffed her bra, or gave blow jobs for money. I heard she lived half the time in France. Sometimes, I'd see her jump from the pier and swim for hours, like a real sea thing, and she would emerge just as she went in: seemingly perfect. There was something about all her fucked-up-ness, always on display, that made me want to wear mine, too.

And then she was always around Otto House.

"Do you even smoke weed?" she asked.

"If I want to," I said.

But that was a lie. I couldn't smoke, and Dad wouldn't allow me to ruin my life with drugs and booze. That's what he told me in his drunkest hours.

"Can you get some?" she asked.

Rook could have collected anything for herself. She spent most of her time alone while her parents did artsy things around the world. She said she feared Dad, though, that he seemed right enough to tell her no, and to rat her out to her parents about smoking so much pot. She was right about that. Dad never let me actually handle any drugs unless it was required.

It was often required.

I knew that Dad kept his own stash in the top drawer of the dresser, under his socks, which were specked with traces of cocaine and smelled like weed. I rifled through his things while Rook peered over my shoulder, hot and breathing down my neck, and then giggling at his perfectly folded boxer shorts. I took a tiny green glob of grass out of a glass pipe, and Rook plucked it from my hand and squeezed it between her fingertips.

"My cousin calls them 'nugs,'" she said.

The way she crushed the tiny nug into little pieces and into a rolling paper, she knew what she was doing. Maybe I did, too. We blew the smoke out the window. We smiled.

"Where's your mom?" she asked.

"Vacation," I said.

Then, on the beach, we made angels by digging our shoulders and the backs of our knees deep into the sand. She told me Dad was hot. That I was beautiful. I felt in love, and we laughed at nothing, and she said I should stay with her for the rest of the summer in her big house, not in a shitty hotel room, or at least until my mom came home. Or until my father came to his senses and fought for Mary. She told me about all her fucked-up-ness, and it was bad, but it wasn't any worse than mine, and there was a sunset, and I told her I was all alone. She curled up next to me, she said she knew what it was like, and she said we'd never be alone again.

This bright shiny thing wanted me. She said it again, that she wanted me forever. That we'd just have to risk it all to belong to each other. She listened to me all night, our hoods wrapped around our heads, and when there was nothing more to say, we fell asleep, buzzed, and woke to the high tide drenching our feet. We carved our names in the sand.

AFTER DAD AND I were kicked out of Otto House for the season, we got a one-month rental close to Rook. My father stumbled home late at night, when the tourists were gone, when there wasn't anybody around anymore to listen to his stories until dawn. Sometimes, they were eerily cool nights, when northern winds brought cold fronts. I could hear his feet fumbling before he found his keys, and that's when I would make Rook leave out the back door. Though she'd often take her time, just to see what a man looked like when he was falling apart.

When he was gone, I sipped warm milk and sifted through piles of history homework, or I watched reruns of Jerry Springer, because he didn't allow me to watch *trash*, or I smoked his weed with Rook on the patio, or I let Rook invite guys from school over to drink cans of his beer.

Dad never knew what time it was when he'd appear foggy-eyed and wasted.

"Why are you still up?" he always asked.

He hated when I saw him like that, and he never had to say it. The shame we both felt for letting all of that happen was a burden only when we admitted the problems. They'd always been right in front of us, but instead, we had to just keep living, because what else was there? His knuckles were often bruised, and a steady trail of blood leaked onto the carpet, the valleys of his knuckles always a bloody map of other men's faces.

"Go to bed," he said.

"You're bleeding," I said.

He squirmed under the crippling fluorescent kitchen light. I carefully bandaged his beaten hands. He whimpered and, through his one good eye, glared at me.

"I'm so sorry, Evie," he said one night—many nights.

Sometimes, his shame felt unbearable.

"Sometimes, I think I'm ruining you," he said.

Sometimes, he was ruining me.

He fell asleep in the chair, and I covered him with a blanket, left the Christmas tree lighted, the window open, because I knew he'd want to wake up to the smell of mainland winter fires. The sea. The island. Salt. I knew that the next morning would be Dad vomiting and saying it was food poison or that he ate something *real, real bad*. That I'd have to make eggs and extrastrong coffee.

"I love you," he whispered.

I never felt unloved, though he was not always capable of defining anything like love, especially during wintertime, when everything felt worse. There was never enough money from the drugs, because he gave them away, lost some, flushed some, or smoked and snorted it all himself.

I slept on the couch next to him, in case he stopped breathing or in case he choked on his own vomit. I wished Rook had stayed.

We ran out of time and money at our late-winter apartment. There was no more drug money to pay. He said it again: *Christmastime is so sad.* We'd speak of the dead dogs and cats, our sorrows, the famed once-snowcapped mountaintop from 1955's winter storm, about *our* dead. Until we had nowhere to go.

Mary married a stout older man who seemed to love Ferry Lands as much as she did, as much as we once did. And the others who'd once let us give them drugs for a place to stay were with their own families on the mainland. Rook sent postcards of paintings from Paris to Otto House until I couldn't collect them anymore when Otto House was boarded for the remainder of winter. No one ever wanted to kick us out, but they all did. Again and again.

Because there was nowhere to go, Dad suggested we camp at the snow peak.

"But we'll freeze," I said.

"But this weather is in your blood," he always said.

I complained of the cold, the walk, the weight of the things we carried on our backs. The island slept, aglow with fires, with warm food and maybe warm hearts, and we climbed quietly up the side of a mountain. I said I wished we'd still had a Christmas tree, or presents, or a home, or another dog, but Dad reminded me that to know the stories of our land was to find the way to happiness. It was at least better than going back to the druggie bunks near the Old Institute.

"But we're fucking homeless," I said.

"It will be an adventure," he said.

The climb took half the night, and when we summited the roundness of the extinct volcano head, we dug our feet into the ground and admired the view. There was the sprawling ocean and the sprawling land, and we were floating above it all. Everything up there soared. Our faces were rosy and chapped. I could feel my heart leaping through my shirt. The sea was thick in wavy blankets of deep greens, and suddenly, the sky looked like it would lick the top of our heads. There was mainland river runoff rushing to the ocean, ships inching along the horizon, the sound of hysterical seabirds. It was cold, but it was all ours, and for a moment, nothing else mattered.

We ate warm wieners and beans, and Dad called us hobos. We played cards again. Dad called us pirates. We drank swigs of whiskey out of paper cups. Dad called us explorers. I wasn't a kid, but we both had to be kids to survive. Under a purple sky of tiny lights, I begged my father to tell me the ecology of our land and our sea and our lives.

Also: "Do you think Mom will ever come back?"

"I don't know," he said.

He took faster sips from the bottle.

We stuffed our sleeping bags with day-old newspapers, and Dad kept a fire going all night. I dreamed of urchins and flames. When the sun shone on the top of the island, we watched every minute of wild illumination, nearly frozen all the way to the pumping organs underneath our skin. Dad made hot tea over the fire. We ate peanuts. I played along with this childish adventure—like it was fun, like we weren't really trapped again—because I didn't want to be the one to kill him.

"Tell me about the time I drowned," I said.

He said it happened when I was only three. Mom was already gone. The sun was low, and it had just rained. I was playing atop slippery rocks, covered in green and blue mosses. He said that in the distance there was a whale's spout and a pod of orcas passing through. He told it like that, with a damp heart of mystery and a crack in his voice. Like it was all magic. I tiptoed on top of the rocks and pointed to the sea. He held my hand until the water erupted with a powerful set of waves, each one stronger than the next, with no time to return to shore. We slipped. We went under. He said it was cold and clear, and there were crisp views of the world beneath. He reached for me, petrified he'd lost the only thing that mattered. But I swam. He said it was as if it were instinct. As if I had been born swimming. My eyes were open, and I swam deeper. I touched the reef below and ran my fingers against pockets of dark weeds. I batted fishes. I twirled up to the surface and pumped my legs like I was a rocket ready to shoot to the moon. He pulled me close, and we rode the next wave in. He said he'd never seen a real smile before, not like the one I wore when I had almost drowned.

I only remember looking up for the light.

WHEN IT WASN'T bone-cold anymore, when people came out of their houses, we were somewhere again. We scrubbed the bottoms of ships for a boathouse with two beds, a sink, a toilet, a hot plate, and a garage door that opened to a quiet expanse of big blue bay.

"I know it's not perfect," Dad said.

"It's fine," I said.

But there was something perfect about a morning bay full of sleeping seabirds.

He'd make more when the tourists came. When the crop came back. When my mother returned.

I drew outlines of bird bodies with a dull-edged pencil on white sheets of paper and waited for something to happen. I drew the snow-covered volcano mouth.

Rook, back from France, came in the night, with warm food, and beers for dad. Said she'd looked everywhere for us, even asked Mary, wondered if we'd found my mother and run off with her to the mainland. She offered us her guesthouse, but my father refused: sometimes, he had pride. We sat around a fire and told ghost stories.

Sometimes, Dad passed out, and we'd take the long way to Rook's place. She'd let me use her nice shower with her nice-smelling bath things, and then we'd stay up all night playing games, sometimes crying, sometimes prank-calling boys, sometimes boozing so hard that she had to hold my hair back. We spent our time doing nothing, but it meant everything. She always woke me before sunrise, and sent me back home, because we agreed it's where I belonged.

Dad was always up early, cleaning things, and I sketched him hammering something into a wall.

"I'm not so good at drawing," I said.

He spread out on the boathouse lawn next to me and half slept while I sketched.

"I guess we are doing our best, little creature," he said.

Earthquake

There was a small tear near the Earth's core, deep below the water that separates Los Angeles from Winter Island. Everything rattled. Things had fallen. My father, too drunk and too high to deal with the moving ground, said it was unlikely we'd get a big aftershock. Unlikely we'd get another big one, because that one had already formed our island. Despite the spooked cats that would not walk with their paws all the way to the ground, he said, we must celebrate my sixteenth birthday. With a limo. With Rook. With the shaken earth.

The limo driver sold weed and speed, but he also owned a furniture store piled high with bright-white lamps and shapely shades and a ceiling made of crystal chandeliers. Said that lighting was his real passion. Inside the limo's hidden pockets were leftover party favors from island partiers: bar swag, a pizza crust, whale-watching ticket stubs, Tin Pan Carnival tokens, and tiny Baggies with traces of white powder.

Dad trusted the speed-lamp-limo guy, of course, through pills and weed buying and selling, as Richie was always one of his most loyal employees. Unlike the rest of the guys, who'd lost their kids to their ex-wives, Richie was just alone. But Richie's druggie loyalty meant I'd be under the strictest supervision, so Dad agreed I could cruise around the island with Rook, drinking as much soda as we wanted, screaming out the windows at tourists, and winking at surfers in their rolled-down-window trucks.

Rook flashed guys as we lapped around the island. Dad often said Rook wasn't welcome at the house, because she would sit inappropriately on the knees and crotches of his friends, because she was always there when I was crying, because I liked her more than I liked him. Because with Rook, I was never alone.

WHEN WE STOPPED at Rocky's Fish N Chips, there were baskets of fried fish and fries, and Dad and his buddies hovering nearby at the bar. Richie poured a Bud from a can into a soda cup and put a lid on it, with a plastic straw. My first full beer from a man, seamlessly passed to me under the table from the lamp-limo driver. Until then, I'd been sneaking sips only when Dad was too drunk to notice.

Dad was so red in the face, blotched and raised with alcoholic red, like a Santa Claus who'd been gulping schooners of cold beers. I must have been red, too. I felt like we were doing something bad being in a bar, and I stuck close to Rook. I watched underage Rook flirting like she knew how to grab a dick. She even rubbed up close on Dad until I dragged her away. We held our shoulders back properly with puffed-out chests, giggling at the late-twenties-to-midthirties druggies and drunks staggering around the bar.

Against the jukebox, and nestled between two smelly trash cans loaded with sauce-stained paper plates, was the youngest of the old-man-bar gang: Bunny. Not thirty yet with long, soft almost-white-blond hair. The tips were almost always crusted with salt after a surf, and he'd stand in the parking lot, wet suit half-off, combing his hair. He'd lie on the hood of his warm truck to dry off, smoking cigarettes for hours. Like it was one long drag.

It was really just the Bud, and his white hair, but I was sure then that I knew what real love was, and I whispered to Rook, *Should I fuck Bunny?* Like I knew how to fuck.

Dad weaseled his way to Bunny, handing him another beer and announcing that it was my sixteenth birthday.

"Get over here!" Dad shouted to me.

Then he did what he always did: explained how well I was doing in math, how my good looks came from my mother, how I was the fastest on the cross-country team at Winter

Island High School, and how I loved animals—especially whales. Like I was always five. Bunny smiled and tapped my Styrofoam cup with his. I sank.

"You're a lucky guy," he said to Dad.

He must have meant that, because when he said it, he actually looked in my direction. Into my eyes. My humiliation about the whales quickly subsided when I felt his arm accidentally brush mine.

Dad rushed to a bar fight up front.

"Your dad says you play sports," Bunny said.

"Cross-country, which isn't exactly a *sport* sport," I said.

Outside, there was light rain. People said it was because of the earthquake—because we blamed everything on earthquakes. Because of earthquakes, things changed. Weather changed. People changed.

Rook was sitting on the lap of Boneyard Rob, a grumpy old guy with grabby hands, and I could tell that Dad was hating every minute of it.

"Get her out of here," he said.

I felt like we were adults, surrounded by drunken old men who rushed home not long after it got dark. Dad was ramping up to an unusually rapid drinking pace, one that allowed him simultaneously to mourn our aging and our collective constant state of regret. He left without saying goodbye, telling the men at the bar that no teenager wanted him around. Rook said she saw him leave. He told me to enjoy the limo, that there'd be time for bars later.

When Richie brought the limo around front, we piled in, our skirts inappropriately flailing around from the storm winds, and we dove headfirst into the back seat. Bunny and the rest of the Rocky's crew waved with boozy giggles. It felt for a second like we were leaving forever, driving away to someplace where these kinds of inappropriate activities didn't exist. That was the moment when I knew it was all wrong, knew I'd have to let it all go, to someday survive, because it's all we could do.

Rook grabbed me and said, *You're so going to fuck that guy.* We had already forgotten that the earth shook.

In the back seat, Rook held my hand so tightly that our fingers were laced together. She said things like she would protect me, save me, make sure Bunny didn't break my heart. Rook knew the things I wished a mother would know. It was hard not to need Rook in this way, to rely on her to tell me things were fine, and then to watch her make my life feel better and bigger. Because for all her lack of mothering, she was strangely perfect at making me feel safe. And alive. Like when we flashed our boobs to the passing ships from the top of the volcano. Like when she stroked my hair as I cried myself to sleep when my father spent the night in jail. Like when she told me I was beautiful.

THERE WAS A bigger earthquake long ago, so colossal that Winter Island shook, too. My mother lived at the epicenter of that mainland earthquake. Pictures fell off walls, hearts rattled, half-full beers fell from dressers, bedside tables, and kitchen counters. The mainland that had lain dormant for years burst alive in excitement and devastation. The news said people were buried.

Her house slid right down the slope of a mountain, and she said everything had dissolved into dust. Her garden, the roots, she said, they remained. Insurance would get her a better home, she said, but until there was something stable, she ferried over with nothing more than a CVS toothbrush and a pack of Hanes panties from the odds-and-ends, diabetic-socks, drugstore-hosiery section. There was some relief that my mother was not lost to the shaking, but some kind of worry, too, that she'd always been able to escape everything.

My father never said a word about her unannounced arrival and instead said things like, *Oh, this is what we do in times of survival.* Or, *You would do the same for me if it were her and you and not you and me, you know?*

Her hair was messy and her skin so pale, and she was the most rattled I'd ever seen her. But there she was, so rattled, and telling me the reason the earth shakes is because of divine miracles, and that tragedies can be miraculous. I was so sick of hearing her talk about how beautiful and magical and spiritual it was for those who can really live on an island. I was sick of hearing her say how much she loved it, too.

My father embraced her during this extended earthquake stay, and he danced with her in the living room light, and I was so annoyed to see him so happy. I was so annoyed that I was so happy, too. At night, my mother smelled like the cool that burrows deep into clothes, and I kept burying my head in her armpit and kept smelling her up as much as I could. Some nights, my mother helped me with multiplication tables. Some nights, I stayed awake listening for the door. Some nights, the news said they'd uncovered bodies.

My mother and father slept in the same bed again, and I could hear her laughing in the night. I was too old to appear in the hallway, fake-scared, but I did it anyway, and she came to my bed and fell asleep next to me, and I wondered whether I'd ever find love in my life and whether it would last forever.

I knew she would leave to go back to the devastation, especially when she showed photos of her mountain house. I felt it suddenly, the coolness in her, and I just blurted out: *When do you go?*

IN THE LIMO, Rook said Boneyard Rob had pinched her butt and then kissed her cheek so close to her lips that it was almost a real kiss. Rook squealed at the rain and opened the sunroof. I was drunk on two beers. Rook pulled a fifth of vodka from her bag, and we drank whatever we could stomach. We leaned back and felt the heat light up our insides.

We squished our bodies together and poked our heads out of the top of the limo, drinking rain like idiot wild turkeys. The streets were flooded, people were worried about aftershocks, and I knew things weren't going to be the same forever; I was too old, and Dad was, too. It wasn't safe anymore to be a daughter and father there.

Rook and I drank warm Buds, and we cracked open cans in the back seat, blasting music and singing our favorite songs. For hours. Richie said if I told about the booze, my father would certainly kill him.

"You're so going to fuck Bunny," Rook said.

I had forgotten, and then, it was all I could think about.

By the time we reached the house, it was pouring. This one was an Italian villa owned by a couple who invented something to do with construction. Dad and I lived there, in the pool house, while its Western Shore owners vacationed in Italy.

Dad had set up all of our camping gear on the great lawn. Drenched, we scurried to our tent and took cover. We braved the rain, lying on our backs and hearing thunder rolling off the other islands in the very far distance. We said no aftershock could reach us there. We started to fade into a dizzying sleep. There was some vodka left, and Rook put the clear plastic bottle to her face, peering through it like she was a fish in a tank.

"Let's go back to the bar," Rook said.

"My dad will know," I said.

But I knew he wouldn't. I knew he was already passed out in the pool house—I saw the light on. Rook and I unzipped the tent as quietly as we could, wearing survival ponchos from the camping box, and escaped out the back gate. We hopped it so the alarm wouldn't go off. I was so agile, so drunk. My legs shook as we ran.

The island was cold and dead, just yellowy porch light through the rain and the deep groan of the foghorn getting louder as we ran along the beach back to the bar. When we arrived, Rocky's was already closed, the sandbags stacked against the front door, and the chain gate down. We didn't need shelter; we needed a thrill. We stopped to breathe, catching our breath over laughter and hysteria, bracing our hands on our knees. We slumped down against the gate, and Rook pulled out a pack of cigarettes.

From the parking lot, a white truck flashed its headlights. I told her I was happy with her. That she was enough.

"It's Bunny," she said.

He flashed them again.

Everything was sinking.

We scurried over wet pavement to Bunny, who was smoking a joint in the cab of his truck with another local guy—a crustie punk who Dad never liked. The sweet scent—of coconut surf wax, wet-suit mildew, and Bunny himself— was intense as we packed into the truck.

Rook already had her poncho off, her skirt hiked up and her body facing the crustie, and Bunny, sweet handsome Bunny, winked at me. He played music on the radio.

"She likes him," he whispered to me.

Rook shook her shoulders to the radio and locked hands with the guy sitting next to her, and soon, she dragged her crustie out into the rain to dance. She looked lovely against the soft streetlights, swaying back and forth, carefully avoiding his tall Mohawk.

Soon, the rain turned to mist, and Rook wandered off with the crustie, and it was just Bunny and me in the front seat.

"You don't have to be so scared," he said.

I had to be terrified. There had been an earthquake.

He draped a blanket across our laps, and we watched Rook and her crustie dance and splash in faraway puddles. Underneath the blanket, Bunny's hand crept to my knee and then up my thigh. He must have known I was near death then, because he stopped and casually took my hand and held it in his. I was spinning from so many Buds, from the way it was all happening without me knowing what was going to happen next, except that it was cold, and sweet, and quiet, and that there was a swipe of blood left over. I don't even remember falling asleep in Bunny's arms.

And then Rook was banging on the windows of the truck, the sun showing atop the sea. Her face was a mess, her eye makeup giving her black eyes. Her punk-rock one-night stand was asleep on the beach, looking like a dead body.

"Your dad will kill us," she said.

I peeled my head away from Bunny's shoulder, and she helped me jump out of his truck. We ran so fast that my poncho turned into a sail, and we laughed. The sand was cold and wet, and there was that smell of crabs washed ashore from the storm. Everything on my insides and outsides felt sore.

When we got to the gate, hopped it, and slid back into our tent, Rook crawled into my sleeping bag and cuddled up next to me. Dad's light was still bright, a sure sign that he was still passed out.

"Did you do him?" she asked.

We were nose-to-nose, and I smiled, still drunk, still confused. We finally fell asleep to the top of our tent spinning under an early morning shower. The cloud cover kept our tent cool, dank and dark, and we slept in longer than usual. When Dad made fake bear noises outside our tent to wake us, I was thankful we'd survived the darkness that night. Inside the pool house, he'd cooked soft scrambled eggs, bacon, and toast, all of which we devoured with our head-pounding hangovers. Dad thanked Rook for coming, for being such a good friend, for *understanding*.

Dad and I folded our sleeping bags on the living room floor, the ones we'd taken from apartment to apartment for all those years. We watched TV together for hours while it rained and rained, slurping chocolate milk and waiting for the weather to get worse so we'd have another reason never to leave.

QUESTION: Describe the world's loneliest whale.

You could end up like the loneliest whale in the sea if you are not careful. If you live on an island with a mother who doesn't want you and a father who wants too much, you might scream and no one will hear you. The kind of mammal who can't even articulate emptiness. If you want to survive, you must learn another language made of mysterious sounds, full of your own answers, and grow a new mouth and a new heart, and keep swimming to the light.

Your father will tell you about the 52-hertz whale, because, he'll say, he's heard her sing underneath the water. He'll say that science says she sounds like a tuba. He calls her Toobie. Scientists have been tracking her songs for a decade, he says, and they say all her songs go unanswered.

Your father will be thrilled by all this unrequited love. The newspaper will slap a front-page rendering of a drawing of a photo of the dark-sea nothingness of this whale on Valentine's Day. Just a lonely whale singing and screaming in a pitch that no other whale can hear.

He will say she sounds like a sinking brass instrument spilling out songs, and that if you put your ear to the ocean, you might hear her for yourself. Except science says that is impossible. Science says you'll need equipment. One day, your father will be gone for the entire day, diving for pearls, and when he returns, his hands will be empty. He'll say he can't remember why he was underwater in the first place. He'll burst into the house, hot with energy, and he'll sway from side to side when he tells you that he *saw* Toobie. *Heard* her. He answered her song.

He'll say: *She's a beautiful, beautiful blue whale.*

Your father will call the scientists from all the institutes, and they'll come to your island for interviews, and they'll stalk your waters for a glimpse, but no one will find the loneliest whale. But he'll tell this story for decades, until you'll believe it, until you tell it, too.

You'll ask your father if it's okay to be that lonely, and he'll say something like: *She's not lonely down there.* You'll ask your father if you will end up like this whale when he dies and if you'll be left with nothing, and he'll say something like: *As long as you have yourself, you'll always have me, and everything else.*

Your father could have heard many things under the water. It's not likely that the 52-hertz whale would have traveled to your island. Yet his story, especially among the drunks and the tourists and the scientists, will be the most credible story you have. Even when science says that this whale that lives alone is lonely, there might be more credible sources that say she's just fine.

FRIDAY

My mother says she dreamed of a dead whale, says it must have been because in those early morning hours when the fire had gone out, when the dogs were restless, thickish fog covered the land and she could smell our whale and hear her actually creaking and rotting out there in the sea.

There are ways to get rid of so-lonely and so-sick whales that have beached themselves at the first sight of land. There are ways that require more effort or less concern. These are the ways my mother takes care of things.

"We can't just burn it up," I say.

"They did somewhere in the seventies," she says.

"Disgusting," I say.

"I think it worked," she says. "You treat all those animals like they're real people."

At the Sea Institute, I talk about great migrations of whales. I like to tell my students that whales always come back. They know the way home. That they can feel loneliness, and most sea mammals don't abandon their young. That I believe them to be almost as human as me.

It's not easy to tell my mother these things, about why I mourn this washed-up body. We don't want to admit the sad things, because it makes us sad.

SHE INSISTS SHE will come with me to run the wedding errands. My mother says it will be hot today, and she cracks the truck window so that a sticky breeze finds our skin. She pulls a thin joint from her purse, lights it, and then asks if I mind if she smokes in my truck. What I mind: my mother, and her filling the space with her space.

"Roll down the window all the way," I say.

My mother and I have smoked pot together before. She likes it with me, she says. She's the one who encouraged my father to grow in our backyard, when we were low on cash, and then to sell it to his fishing buddies. She's the one who first explained to buyers that it was fresh and organic and that the island soil made it unlike any other weed on earth. She was the one who called it Winter Wonderland. By the time she left, we had no cash, and Dad was growing wild weed in planters alongside our sunlit garage. And then more.

She hands me the joint, and we are smoking together, and I think that my lips have touched the same paper as hers and it's the closest we've ever been, though she's sitting right next to me and claims that I once lived inside her very body cavity.

She gets a little rush, a soothing one, and she talks the whole way, even when she's filling her lungs with more smoke. She talks through everything—the radio, a fire truck, the roar of circus sounds and arcade explosions from Tin Pan Carnival.

I wonder if she is aware of the little space left between us on the bench seat, and if she's just filling it up with pointless conversation to make it all easier for her. Also, this: it is easier when she talks.

"Do you remember that house?" I say and point.

Along the gloomy heap of cramped beachside bungalows is the house where I was born. The woman who pulled me from my mother's legs was a biologist who looked after the sea mammals at the Old Institute. She said my birth wasn't so far from a seal's, anyway. My mother said I came quickly, before there was time to get a ferry, and even that would have taken too long in the storm, because there I was, like a wet fish covered in blood and mucus, in the care of my mother, my father, and, for a few hours, a marine biologist. Our small hospital clinic is only open for routine daily hours (for tourists who drunkenly fall off bikes and balconies and break bones). In case of emergency, we transport people back to the mainland. It's still undecided what an emergency is in my life.

My mother is offended now. She's moving around in her seat, and the joint's done, so she moves on to a cigarette. She never likes my tone. My tone says that I think she's a broken mess and that it's her fault that I'm broken. Also, she's overreacting.

"I am the one who gave birth to you, who carried you for what felt like years, and breastfed you, and put you to sleep, and wiped your ass, and of course I fucking remember that house," she says.

I wish I could remember myself as a baby. I wish I could swim outside of myself and watch my mother holding, and rocking, and feeding, and bandaging skinned knees. But the memories of her are faint, and I can only remember a few things with clarity: late-1980s movie soundtracks, her fast-forwarding through the sheer-white-curtain sex scene in *Top Gun*, and that as a child, I believed I *was* a seal.

I try to parallel-park the truck, and she suggests that there must be a closer spot. She tells me to keep looking, and I can't speak up because I have "Highway to the Danger Zone" stuck in my head, so I continue to drive around to look for a better space.

"Why don't I just drop you off in front," I say.

"I'm not a fucking crippled old woman," she says.

My mother is still beautiful. Sometimes, people say we are sisters, and when it happens, I feel like maybe I'm dying. She's kept her hair long and dyed dark brown, her skin is mysteriously nice and tan, from some kind of lineage we've never found, and her clothes fall well against her in all the right ways. She loves cheap jewelry, and she laces herself with fake shine, though she doesn't need it, because somehow, despite the horror of her unmotherliness, she is bright from within. Yes, from the fucking inside.

Today, my mother looks perfect, in cutoff jeans and a pink T-shirt. I'm wearing a sweater practically made of dog hair and my fingers reek deeply of fish guts. My skin is always beaten by wind and sun, and my shoulders are too big, my torso too short. But my hair is long and dark, like hers.

"Please just let me drive," I say.

She shouts that someone is leaving up ahead, and I speed to the empty space. I hate speeding. Before I can turn off the engine, my mother is on the curb and directing the tail of my truck into the spot. She is the kind of woman who gets out of a moving vehicle.

"You're a little far from the curb," she shouts.

I tell her to pay the meter, but she claims she's got no cash, no coins, nothing. It must be a big purse full of lipsticks, smokes, and gum. I take deep breaths, but my mother is there to disrupt those, too. She loops her arm in mine, like we are some kind of woven-together mess, and she prances me to the tailor. Already, I'm dreading the whale, the wedding, my mother, how the island people will talk of my mother and her coming back again, and their guessing game of how long she will stay. They will take bets. *And where is Liam?*

Here, in this small blue-carpeted room lined with dry cleaning and sewing machines, they have known me for years. Don and Sujin own the bait shop near the harbor, where they have let me squeeze living worms into Styrofoam cups. They have also bought up a ton of Western Shore vacation homes and spend most of their time traveling and sending their kids to college with all their money. My father has rented their garages and apartments over all the years. They know my mother—know her absences, too.

My mother is on her best behavior when Don unlocks the door. She's instantly charming, and Don smiles at the sight of her. Everyone does. Don must not suspect we are high, though as I glance to my mother, I see that her eyes have been licked with pink glaze. She won't let go of my arm, even when she kisses Sujin on the cheeks—left then right— and Sujin giggles. I smile, too. What else can I do?

Don appears with a dress in a bag, zipped up like there's a second body of mine in there, and my mother seems elated. She unleashes me from her grip and focuses on Sujin, telling her how lovely the store is, how wonderful the island is for a wedding, and how profoundly lovely Sujin looks after all these years. Says, *Koreans don't age.* My mother grasps Sujin's forearms with her hands and keeps up with her compliments. Worse, Sujin is blushing. My mother says *lovely* again. She is high as fuck.

"You know I sell Marine Nutrition creams, the overnight ones, that are truly the best," my mother says. "Made from real jellyfish."

My mother pulls the tubes and lubes from her purse, rubs the creams on Sujin's hands, her arms, and massages them into her skin.

"You look lovely, really," my mother says again.

My mother winks at me while I'm holding the body bag.

Don was always loyal to my father. He tries to disentangle Sujin from my mother, insists that she help me get into the dress, or get the dress out of the bag, or do something away from my insane mother and her sea creams. He can tell by my series of uncomfortable expressions that I need my mother far, far away.

"You two could be sisters," he says. And he winks.

WHEN I APPEAR from behind the curtain, everyone's face goes white and then pink and then red, and there is some kind of electric burst of emotion. Sujin's hands, so soft now, hold mine, and my mother runs to hug me. Don claps his hands together a few times and says I'm beautiful, that my father would say so. When I look in the mirror, I see a woman wearing a dress, and it might not be me. I wish that I wasn't so high. I wish for Liam and our life away from things like my mother, and my dead father, and reminders of things which we don't want to be reminded of. Liam would tell me that the dress is perfect, even if I feel stupid.

There are grizzly bears in Alaska that will eat a beached humpback whale. It's the only time they'll share a meal. The only time they will not fight over food. The only time they are peaceful among one another—so full, resting in the shallows of the cool Pacific Ocean after their feast. My mother tells me this while we're in the drive-thru sandwich shop, the only drive-thru on Winter Island. She doesn't stop talking, my mother, because she's nervous I might speak up, say the things I want to say, like, *Why are you here? Please go away.* She keeps talking until there's no room to say anything.

I pay the woman the heaps of found change in my mother's never-ending purse, after all. My mother shouts a joke that we can't afford to pay in dollar bills through the driver's-side window. The sandwiches are wrapped in paper and stuffed in long paper bags, and my mother lays them across her lap.

"They're hot," she says.

"I told you we got hot sandwiches," I say.

"But I didn't realize they were hot," she says.

We are familiar with the front seats of cars. My mother and I have spent many years sitting together, strapped in, wheels beneath our feet, trapped in a metal box that goes fast. The only escape are the windows, the breeze, and the real-life sounds that trickle into the body of these cars, and then there's no real escape at all. It feels like the rising heat of the meat on her lap is taking over. We are in a box of hot pastrami, and I want to pull over. She says not to roll down the windows so the dress doesn't blow out; she says the dress will smell like pastrami if we don't roll down the windows.

"You're awfully quiet," she says.

She says it every time.

"What do you want to talk about?" I say.

"I shouldn't have to tell you what to talk about. You should just want to talk to your mother," she says.

So I bring up the sandwiches. Liam would tell me to tell her to fuck off. Or tell me to drop her off somewhere and tell her to not bother again unless she's going to be decent. I tell her I'm mad that she thought she was getting a cold sandwich when I had already explained that the sandwiches are hot. I keep going, keep driving, keep talking about those pastramis on her lap. The dress in the bag sways from the small hook in the nearly nonexistent back cab of the truck.

She's quiet. She keeps adjusting the sandwiches and shifting them as they get hot against her skin. She gazes out the window. This is not about sandwiches.

"I guess that's a start," she says.

We stop at that park that overlooks the entirety of the sunlit harbor, and we sprawl out on a filthy picnic table covered in white gull shit. It's windy. We need sweaters. We don't have them, but I have a beach towel in the truck bed. It smells like seaweed and fish. And now pastrami.

I ask my mother if she wants to protect her ass from splinters and shit, or if she'd rather wrap herself in the towel.

She takes our sandwiches and plops down on a patch of lawn, her bare legs already stuck to the half-dead grass, and wraps the towel around her shoulders. Then she opens the rest of the dirty blue towel like a wing, and motions for me to get in.

I say I'm not cold, and we eat the hot sandwiches on the lawn, where I'm surely getting eaten by grass fleas and breaking out in some kind of rash. She swoops open her wings again and finally, I crowd into the side of her body. She's quiet when she eats, so I eat slowly and hope she follows.

It's easy to forget about the whale here, and for a moment I free myself of the thought that Liam is gone. The sandwiches are good. The wind turns to breeze. My mother and I are in a blue blanket under blue sky near big blue sea. Only for a moment can I let myself be swallowed by the romance of my mother and a wedding and true love, and a father who made me feel loved. And a mother, too, who says she loves me. I desperately want to tell her, or someone, that even though I'm getting married in a few days, I'm not sure I know how to make love last forever. Or at all.

I want to talk about my father. About how my life didn't turn out the way I thought it would, the fact that I wasn't sure how it was supposed to turn out, that I'm bound to a rock in the sea, that I might not know how to be in love, that I might not know what love is. That my mother, and my father, and the storms, the mountains, the mainland, my own mothering—that it might have ruined everything. I want to talk about Liam. About our most-of-the-time happiness, how I'm afraid I'll lose him someday, too, because I don't know what it's like to keep things. My mother is still eating. She keeps on with the silence, and I'm so pained by the nothingness between us, the momentary peace, that I have to break it, because sometimes I don't know what else to do but break things. To find the chaos.

"Dad used to bring me up here after school," I say.

"There's not one inch of this island that your father didn't know," she says.

She talks about the wedding. Will there be flowers? How many people? Did we hire people? The dogs will be in the wedding, too? Why not a church? And more. She's put so much value on something I never cared about, and for a moment, it's easy to play along; it's easier than talking about the things that broke us.

The things that broke us: the harshness of the earth, and love.

I ask my mother how many men she's loved. She says she can't keep track. She asks how many men I've loved. I say one. She laughs like a maniac, and she opens her arms, her wings, and wind hits us in the chest.

She tells me I'm sweet and begs me to tell her how I met Liam, and how I knew he was, as she's kept saying, *the one*. She tells me I'm so tough but so soft, and I hate that she calls me soft, so I unravel myself out of her grip and stretch out on the grass. My life is everyone else telling me who I am or how I feel.

There are birds waiting for food and pecking the grass for nearby leftovers. She swats them away. She tells me to calm down, that she's only kidding, and musters up this: *I'm happy for you.* She begs me again to tell her how I met Liam.

"On the docks," I say.

"Oh, come on. There's more to it," she says.

"He was really funny, and he asked me for a drink, and then we walked on the beach, and, I don't know, we've just been together ever since," I say.

She talks flowers again.

I MEET LIAM under end-of-summer light. He appears, disheveled, from a boat that wandered into the wrong harbor with urgency, full of fresh fish. He's the one who shouts the tuna count from the bow. We say that if that boat's engine hadn't failed, he would be dead, or would be farther south like he had charted, would be another's and a great unknown.

He stays at Otto House for at least a week and waits for the engine parts from the mainland. I drop off flyers in the lobby for the Sea Institute's summer camp, and peeking above a newspaper is his messy blond hair.

Rook is behind the front desk, and she'd said something about a beautiful man who washed up with all that hair, and he's sitting right there, and he's totally fuckable. She'd said she was going to invite him out and that he's quiet. She'd said he was perfect for me.

He folds his newspaper the wrong way, a new line making a new, wrong half, and before he leaves, Rook shouts to him, and he approaches the desk. Everything like we are sixteen again. She says something like, *This is Evie. She's just moved back here, and she's a native, and she loves giving tours of the island. Twenty bucks.*

We sort it out, that I don't want his money but that somehow he wants the tour, and he asks if that little boy running around is my kid or hers. *Hers*, I say. *And mine.*

I take Liam out for hours in a golf cart, even to the Old Institute, and I tell him that my father is dead, that I once thought I was a seal, that I've never really been in love, that I'm bound to the island forever. I say almost everything, and that I hoped that he'd get his engine parts, get back to fishing, find his life back on the mainland. But he says, *I like it here.* Says he always wanted to be a fisherman. Always wondered about islands.

We are exactly one year and three days apart, and we try to figure out if soon we will be twenty-seven at the same time, but we cannot do the math. And his eyes are the kind that see into me, through me, around me, and he knows me. I tell myself there is no explanation for this feeling. I tell myself that it's biology. Or desperation. Cabin fever.

I keep saying these things when he moves his things into my bungalow on Ferry Lands. When we get the dogs. When we plant a garden. When he writes me poetry. When Tommy moves in because Rook's gone again. And he just keeps loving me. For no reason except that he does. And I don't ask, because I'm afraid to really know, and afraid it might not be real.

I can never say how much I love him. Not even to myself, because I'm always waiting for him to leave. When he makes himself go cross-eyed after telling a joke—there are so many good jokes—or when he says he'd live on the highest mountain with me or the smallest island, I just can't say it. Because how could I know how to say those kinds of things?

I've been living my life hoping that the blue wings of a mother mean true love. I spend my waking hours looking for answers in the patterns of sea creatures who cannot speak. Liam is the first to tell me that he inconsolably loves me. And, perhaps it's some kind of tidal pull, or the light side of the moon, or that the sun is a fucking hot star, but there's no one I could ever love more.

EVEN WITHOUT REASON.

Autumn

For the first decade of our marriage, Liam lives most of his life at sea, staring at sunsets and catching fish for cash. When he returns each season, we must start again. We curiously examine one another's faces, against the wind and the lines, against the sinking and the sagging. We rush together, exhausted by loneliness and months of fear that love will never return, only to meet again, our bodies sighing in relief. We continue on.

The woods are still, and the nighttime temperatures dwindle, and the trees shed their leaves. There is a smell this time of year as everything starts to dry up, and sometimes we dry up, too. We are intertwined in our bed, and sometimes, one of us is slumped over, asleep in a chair, and the other reading on a couch. I often worry that he loves the time on the boat more than he loves me.

When his ship is late, I scan the horizon from the top of the lighthouse, with the roundness of binoculars suctioned to each eyeball, watching boats teetering into the harbor, all of them carrying everyone else's husbands and not mine. Those storms, the ones that come to pass, make me feel as if the moment of pouring-down rain or insufferable wind will break the windows. Will break my heart. And I wait. I feed the dogs. Tommy needs help with his science-fair project, so Rook passes him to me, and she drinks wine and sits on the front porch. There is the putting of seeds in dirt and the waiting for them to grow into something that gives air. Then he arrives, his hands colder than before, and before he showers, he kisses my face and he says the things I want to hear: *Oh, how I've missed you.*

For a stretch of the season, he's home, and we busy ourselves with our hands: We make food, pick and prune, run our fingers alongside the parts of our bodies that peek from our clothes. We make love, we sing with fake-microphone hands, and, sometimes, we cry with our faces pressed up against our palms.

Then we make the terrible kind of mistakes. We disobey our own rules.

"I'll never do it again," he says.

"But how could you tell me?" I say.

"It was just a mistake," he says. "Only a few times," he says.

But I'm not angry that he's touched another woman with the same hands that rest upon my hip in the night, the hands that scrub my back in the shower. I'm angry that he's told me and broken his vow to keep me away from that kind of hurt. We said, *What happens to us while we are away does not belong to us.* Because we never agreed to be faithful, but we did agree to keep each other from ruin.

And then, "Do you love her?"

He must have at least loved her at low tide, when he was off living life as another person. I, too, have lived many lives, and when he's away, I am a full-time researcher for the Sea Institute, I am a part-time lecturer, I am a part-time mother to Rook's child, a part-time daughter, friend, drinker, sinner, griever, and now, a woman with new hobbies.

When he goes, I can be whoever I want to be, and I have slept with others, too. But in his great returns, we have always learned to find ourselves together again. So when he tells me there's a woman off the coast of San Francisco who has hair radiant like the sun and twin daughters and a husband who'd vanished at sea, I can't piece it all together enough to understand why he's betrayed me by sharing this other life. It hurts too much. Our life can be confined to this island, its happiness and sadness. Now, the disruption of betrayal.

"You are selfish to tell me this," I say.

"I thought you'd want to know," he says.

"What for?" I say. "Because you want me to divorce you?"

He tells me the things that have hurt him: He says I never really need him. That I don't let him need me. That I'm harsh like the wind and I say things that make him think that I might never really love him, or perhaps it's that I don't say anything at all. Says he's felt lonely, and we try to decipher the difference between *lonely* and *alone*. Sometimes, he wishes things were simple, he says, but I think what he means is that he wishes I was easier to love.

Except, I explain after we are drunk, that he is the one holding back, that he is the one who wants to be with a boat, and another woman, and another life. I tell him that he can't deal with himself, with all of his past pain that has so slowly revealed itself over time until we are here and we are both lonely.

He's not the kind of person to believe in a lifetime of grief, or that the loss of people and things makes him susceptible to ache. He is the kind of person who says he's better now because of that past. Says things like: *I have to keep moving.* And I'm drunk, and I scream that I can't fix his heart if he doesn't believe his is beating.

I shut him out, spending my time in my research, making notes on answers I've promised to find:

- The ocean is relatively shallow from a planetary perspective.
- Can you have this perspective?

THESE MONTHS WE'VE spent part apart have led to years of new interests, like throwing pottery, dressage, baking. He's missed the dreadful foggy summer mornings and hot windy afternoons. He's missed the fires on the mainland that glow from faraway hills. He's missed Tommy learning to love Rook again and calling us both Mom, and the man that Rook punched in the face after he'd cut Tommy from the basketball team, and then there was a red tide that washed up things we hadn't found in years. He's missed me flirting with a bald scientist, the a-little-more-than-a-kiss behind the lab. Missed it never meaning anything, just like I promised it wouldn't. And we promised to keep these secrets. We are good at saying nothing and pretending.

I ask him if he has felt any pain or if he is only concerned with the mechanics of catching fish, and he says that keeping his hands busy helps him bury anything that hurts. I wonder if he'll ever know how to be with himself. To be with me. It's wild to tell him that I hope he's burning when he returns again, to beg him to at least try to think of the sadness. Hoping he'll need me to remind him of where to find the joy.

Each time he returns, we say things like: *I've never loved anyone the way I love you,* and also, *I'm not sure how we just keep doing this.*

The first few days he's back, we are infants, rolling around like lops with confused brains, finding ourselves and our way back to one another. Then with the silence, I feel tired of love. Sometimes, there's raunchy sex, and some-times, a nighttime full of tears.

There are the scheduled plans that have been on the cal-endar for months. The things we have been doing together for years: the Winter Island Lemon Festival, dinner with friends at Otto House, big waves from direct south swells, and, this year, Tommy's twelfth-birthday party. There is surf fishing for dinner and cooking on top of an open fire, tending to Ferry Lands together. Once, building a treehouse, and once, training a new puppy. The years, though, with the weathering of things, get harder and longer, and Liam begs that we schedule fewer things and spend more time tak-ing naps near one another and by the sea. Just being near. Sometimes, I think he's come home burning, and sometimes I just don't know. Still, it feels good when he is near, despite my anger.

On the porch are pails of the shells that came with the red tide. We sift through them together. Liam says he wishes he could have seen it. He tells tales of the coast of California, the bitter cold that came too early. He says that the fish were farther south this year, because the waters are changing and moving. He says it's warmer here, and that all sharks will come to feed in our harbor. He says we should keep a look-out from the lighthouse. He makes me watch *Jaws*, and we eat an entire gallon of store-brand ice cream, and we fuck all night by the fire, and he pretends his hand is a shark fin on top of his head. It's that things are good with Liam; they are peaceful, and fine, and happy. And though there's some sadness, the living of other lives, it's that when he's home, everything feels wonderful. Especially when I don't think of betrayal.

We misjudge the distance to Rook's place and get there sooner than we expect. We are distracted by the truth and can't gauge how far away things really are. Liam is surprised at how close her new place is to ours. He pulls me close, in the eve of darkness, and asks if I think she'll stay for Tommy this time, if Tommy is happy with her, if she'll take him away again.

"I don't know," I say.

We are early enough to help her with the filling up of blue-and-white balloons, and she instructs Liam to tie the balloons to the backs of chairs. Rook makes guacamole in the kitchen, and when her parents arrive, there is a sigh of peace. Her house is big and empty, like her parents' house was, and Tommy's got his own room, and there's a swimming pool. Her mother thanks me for looking after Tommy when Rook is away—all the times she's been away—and Liam says we don't mind. I know what it means to leave people.

Tommy acts cool at this age. He and his friends avoid the adults and hang out by the twinkling lights lining the pool. It's too cold to swim, but one of the obnoxious friends jumps in wearing his clothes. Rook is frazzled, and her parents remind her about all the terrible things we've done in their hot tubs. A few other mothers join the adult table, and we snack on what Rook's left out: cheese and vegetables and chips and guac. There is wine, and Tommy, who's stayed dry, hugs me from behind, and he tells me he loves me. Liam squeezes my hand, and Rook, who has never been heartbroken about me and her son, tells me she loves me, too.

There are the conversations we have together as husband and wife, and then the outward conversations we have with strangers, and both, even after a party as intimate as Tommy and his shitty friends managing to survive junior high school, are equally hard. Tonight, we carry around a secret: Liam might love someone else, and now we know, and now we must pretend not to think of lips on lips, under the same moons, near the same ocean. I wonder what I would really tell him. And if I was capable of hurting him the way he's hurt me.

"Can we pick a few avocados from your tree this week?" Rook asks.

Liam nods, his teeth wine-purple. Exhausted from playing nice in front of others. But we agree to take the longer way home, the one where we must walk the majority of Ferry Lands to get to the bungalow, where the dogs are howling at the sound of our feet rolling on rocks on our way up to the door.

We say very little. There is the moon—it's full—and our upcoming obligations. We agree that we are tired. Maybe always tired. But tonight, we say, we are full. There is more to say, but after many years, we've learned that saying the things doesn't always clean up a mess. So we say we still love each other, and maybe we mean it, and there are half smiles. I bury my face into his chest when he holds me. What if we've evolved into something entirely new?

- Life forms from nothing.
- Aristotle: Life arises out of nonliving organic material, miraculously.

A FEW WEEKS together, and Liam's body is tired. He says it's the years at sea. There's pain in my back, too. Everything is not as it once was; my ass is rounder and falling to the earth, and I show him by lifting up the back of my robe. He laughs, and reaches for me. The years of sleeping quietly with our hair smashed onto the same pillow has caused neck pain. Liam says his urges are different now, that maybe in all the years, we have shed so much sunburned skin it's all just flaked off into the air and the sea, and that now we are entirely new people. Yet for all our shedding, and all that's left, I wonder if we can still find love.

"Is it strawberry lemonade this year?" he asks.

This year, I have not yet made the lemonade for the Winter Island Lemon Festival. There are baskets of strawberries and baskets of lemons. There are cutting boards and knives. And there's nothing but lying in bed and wondering about the other woman, whether there have been more, whether I should have called Bunny on lonely nights, or my college boyfriend, whether I should have lingered in a bar, whether I should have never let Tommy go, whether I should have ever married Liam. Whether I'd ever really be able to let Liam go. Whether I've already let him go. The truth is that I stopped sleeping with other people years ago and I quietly committed to Liam. I wonder why I didn't say it.

"I'm already so behind," I say.

"Fuck it, let's just skip it," he says.

When he kisses my mouth, his tongue feels like someone else's tongue. We could lie around Ferry Lands all day, and throw the ball for our dogs, and walk on the beach, and revel in our peace and in our unknowing, and there would be some kind of pleasure in it all. He unties my robe. But there is a sense of duty and responsibility that comes with being a part-time woman; I must make the strawberry lemonade and stand behind the booth and talk to old men about my father, while Liam plays catch with Tommy, and Rook is wiping down our table and taking cash donations for the Sea Institute. I swat his hand from my ass. He asks, *So are we okay?*

In the kitchen, Liam cuts the green off the strawberries and eats fleshy chunks as he goes. I squeeze lemons into a bowl and accidentally wipe sting into my eyes. He dares me to lick a lemon, and I dare him to squeeze one into the open cut on his arm. Sometimes, in the mundaneness of happiness and constant unknowing, I want to ask Liam about that other woman's nose, her lips, her ass, but it's only because I know how to break things. Sometimes, I wonder what we would be like if we were mainlanders, driving in traffic, too exhausted every night to talk or fuck, working the kind of backbreaking work that doesn't ever require your back. We talk of this life sometimes, and there were years where we thought we could try it, because we think we can try it anywhere. But there was Tommy and Rook and my mother. Our lives have become uncomplicatedly complicated. Maybe we don't really know what we want.

"What if you end up loving her more than me?" I say.

He squeezes a drop of lemon juice into the air.

"Do we have to do this?" he says.

Sometimes, I want to do this. Sometimes, we do this.

- What does it mean to love other people, each other, ourselves?
- Is it possible to love everything at once, and sometimes love nothing, too?
- The ocean is made of invisible layers of floating particles that move without intent, but they keep moving anyway.

THERE ARE PAPERS and charts, with plotted points, with the trails of sea life, and dull-edged pencils and all the erasure shavings. I work at the drafting table most of the day.

When Liam appears, he has hot tea and he gently closes the window. The office window is a picture of the ocean, and when there's the vastness of light peering inside, I must draw the blinds. Without Liam, there is routine and ritual, and when he's home, there is all that light. Without Liam, work is easier, and I know I'll find answers.

"What are you working on?" he says.

He sits in the comfortable chair, the one near the window, with the overgrown snake plants that press into the chair's leather back.

"Migration, still," I say.

There is something simple about migrating and then coming back. I've told him this before, and he says he knows it, too. And he says, *We keep coming back*.

"Are you still mad?" he says.

"Yes," I say.

He asks if he can stay anyway, to read in the chair by the end-of-day window light while I mark plot points on intertidal charts and tally last season's whales to make predictions for next year.

I never answer, but he's there, and we are soon forgetful of one another's presence, at least by the sound of it. There's something there, even in the deep-down fury and deep-down forgiveness that lingers. Eventually, I ask him to close the shade, and there is another distraction: dinner.

"Do you think we should take one of those couple's cooking classes?" he said.

We have this conversation most often. More than our madness about who does the most laundry, or who walks the dogs longer, or who kisses other people. More than those, there's this one, the one where he pushes me to piece together a broken thing, because as he says, I'm the one who can do it.

There have been years of research I've collected for the Sea Institute, and while he's away, lectures and advisees, trustee and funding parties that require tight dresses and high heels. Still, I have never actually looked into a couple's anything for us. I wonder if that's what's holding us back.

"I just get so busy," I say.

Our bookshelves are littered with old photos of us: Tommy, our lives, our pets, our fathers, and our mothers. When we are drunk and sloppily eating bowls of cereal before bed on Friday nights, we laugh that we've kept all these memories so long. Sometimes, Liam says it's a miracle that we found each other.

We feel a pull back to the sea, even before he must leave again on his next charter, because desire is always there and our walks expand to the longer paths. The days are shorter, and then there is our time together catching ferries to the mainland to visit Home Depot, and making dinner for Tommy while Rook is at work, the hikes to the volcano, the shower sex, the waterproof rain gear to slosh around in the low tide, the shouting, the middle-of-the-night crying, and all the other things that slowly take up the speeding up of time and the water that keeps moving.

I want new rules but can't think of how to ask unless it's a beg. He hates disruption, he says, and I say: *So then what are we doing?*

"I'll miss you most," he says.

At night, I wonder whether I should be angrier, whether I'm incapable of saying how I feel or, worse, whether I'm incapable of feeling how I feel. I roll him over when he's snoring and hope he'll wake, abandon his sleep, and talk with me and let me scream and fight. But this is my husband, a man who cannot read minds, a man who is every other man. I push my fingers into his back, so gently, to nudge him to turn on his side. This time, there is some unexplainable act of mind reading, nuisance, or holiness, and he says, *I can't get comfortable.*

The nights are so long before he leaves, and we stay awake, waiting for the day to come, and we say everything until every word has lost its meaning. We talk and talk until we hate one another and then love one another again. He tells me his fears, for the first time in a decade: that he thinks we are wasting away, that he misses the ones he's loved and lost, that if he cries once, will it ever stop? We say all the things we've wanted to say, like, *I would never do this to you* and *But in your own way, you have done this to me.* We promise we won't shut it off, shut it out, exist like nothingness. We promise to feel the pain so we can feel ourselves again. We also promise to cherish the nothingness. We say we'll just keep promising.

Winter

We collect trinkets that remind us of all our mistakes and display them on shelves so we don't forget. Constant reminders that science won't explain the complicatedness of our love. The uncertainty. Before we were married, we must have felt this way, but there's so much of the unknowing in our bones. When he returns again, we aren't speaking, because time has passed, and I haven't received any letters, and my imagination has taken hold. When he returns, he wants things to be the same.

"But you said you've forgiven me," he says.

But how could I forgive you?

Night comes early during the season of our namesake, and Liam is home every day. There is no work at sea, and we eat our food sparingly so we won't have to do something drastic together, like shop for more food. Each day, there are pockets of wet drool on the pillowcases that I must wash. I make excuses to get to the mainland. Until he knows what I'm doing. Until he knows I'm always trying to leave. Though I don't say it. I've been putting my things together slowly, like I'm in a play, and the audience must know that I'm going away.

Because there has been time. Enough of it that there has been a lunar eclipse. A dog has had a thorn wedged between the softness of paw. There have been minutes where the white noise began to sound like a song. Where loneliness, the kind island people dread, poked her head. There was enough silence to feel abandoned. To imagine his body on hers, on someone else's, with better hair and tits, nicer feet, with the kind of laughter that is contagious. Enough time to look at the lines in the mirror and wonder if making it out alive was worth all the pain.

The whales were scarce, and I want to tell Liam what waiting feels like. What staring at a straight line looks like. That I was nothing without him, but the unbearable pain of waiting, of wanting, of not being able to ever tell him anything, was making me feel tired. That by another return, I'd be a shriveled sea witch. I want to tell him that I have to push him away. First. To prevent the kind of damage that breaks windows and tears apart homes. But the days pass, there are more hours, and the right things to say flee. Then it feels like just me again.

"Can't you just stay a few more hours?" he says. "I'm hoping for snow on the volcano."

My excuses are weak: the Sea Institute needs me, a porpoise will be born, I am doing a lecture, I'm tired, I would like to visit my mother. The real reasons: I'm not sure he loves me like I love him. And I can't bear the thought of loving him anymore. Each day, the burden of that brokenness feels bigger.

"Don't forget to take the dog to get his allergy shot," I say.

"How long will you be gone?" he asks.

But how can I know? I am still mending all my bleeding things.

"Not long," I say.

He packs me a paper-sack lunch, and I eat the frozen grapes on the ferry. I hope he begs me to stay.

• An ocean's ecosystem becomes resilient and
   develops the capacity to recover from disruption.

MY INSTINCT IS to go to my mother. To what ought to be solid ground. To ask her for approval. To make her tell me things are okay, that Liam is a great love, to hold me close without saying anything, to take me to lunch and talk about her favorite HBO shows. My mother never delivers on any of these things, but she certainly loves to be needed. These moments of brokenness seem to make her feel better about herself, her life. These chances make her feel like a mother again.

I never feel like a daughter.

I drop a folder of papers in a mail slot at the Institute and drive north to Ventura, where my mother lives a quiet life on a chicken farm. She's spread out in a plastic Adirondack chair, with her bare legs stuck and baking in the sun, drinking a giant cup of iced something, her lips swiped Revlon red. She greets me like there have been years of forgiveness. She asks why I've come unannounced and then doesn't let me answer. She's holding a basket of eggs, and there's a chicken feather stuck to her hair.

"Please take some eggs back to Liam," she says.

She scoots me to the rest of the lawn furniture, where I'm to take my pick of plastic chair to sink into. It's sweltering, but there's a view of the mountain, and a breeze coming in from the sea.

"You moving in?" she asks.

"I have some Institute stuff I have to do this week," I say.

"You usually stay there," she says.

She hands me a sip of her spiked iced tea and says she knows a face like mine, and that last night she had a dream of a hurricane and she knew there was trouble, because the air smelled like salt. She knows everything, is what she's really saying, and there's some perceived sick delight that I can't help but hate her for. And still, I need her to tell me that everything will be okay.

"Did you fuck someone else?" she says.

A wave of red anger hits like fiery sun, and I rip my legs off the chair and stand, and I intend to leave and run off like a kid, and shout, scream in her face, but I don't do anything but feel the heat inside.

"*He* did," I say.

"Well, what did you expect?" she says.

I start my fast stampede to the car, and I'm proud of the dust that's trailing.

"Evie, I'm sorry, but are you telling me you have never loved another person besides Liam?" she says.

"He doesn't love her," I shout back.

"Then why are you so angry?"

"It's selfish that he told me."

She peels up out of the chair, and the crooked back screen door squeaks and slams shut.

I sit in my car, hands on the wheel, foot on the gas, but the engine is off. I stare at the dirt path that leads to the paved road that leads to the massive concrete freeway that divides the mountains and ocean. Then there is the Sea Institute and the ferry back to the small vastness of an island. And I don't leave.

She appears with a shorter glass with more booze and less tea, and slides into my front seat.

"Does he know?"

"Know what?" I ask.

"How much he's hurt you."

We sit in silence, windows down, and sip cocktails while a few scraggly chickens meander down the path ahead. We can smell them in this heat. She reclines her seat slightly and puts her feet on the dash and asks if I want to stay for dinner, and I make a rude remark that I have nowhere else to go, and she finally says something a mother should say, but it's not enough:

"But there are so many people who love you."

- The rates of ecosystem recoveries vary.
- Recovery depends on severity.
- Sometimes an organism must play a different ecological role under pressure.

FOR A FEW days, I tend to the chickens and the kale, and we spend hours in the sun. When it cools at night, we wrap ourselves in scarves and lament this early December heat wave. The chores combat the loneliness. We spend hours drunk and high. We spend nights in town and order food in broken Spanish on the north side. Liam calls a million times. There are Christmas trees for sale in parking lots. My mother says her new boyfriend left her for another woman, and there were probably more. There are so many eggs: scrambled, boiled, poached with hollandaise. I enjoy the faking of happiness with her, because sometimes, I can be happy with her.

When Liam calls my mother's house again, she tells him I'm there, but I'm out, somewhere wandering the land or in town. More calls, and then she tells me this is no way to be a wife, and finally, after a few beers I tell her that she doesn't have any idea how to be a wife or a mother or a woman. I even throw my glass against the concrete patio. It shatters, and she gets a broom and repeats herself: *This is no way.* She tells me to go home to my husband, to my life, to the things I love, because otherwise I'll be an old woman alone on a chicken farm.

In the morning, there's a note, and Advil and Gatorade: *I'm sorry that I've hurt you for so many years, but you aren't me, and you are better.* My mother is pulling greens from her garden boxes in the backyard, and the morning is mild but the sun is strong, and her floppy hat covers her face, and she waves.

"There's a few cartons of fresh eggs to take home," she shouts.

• Pieces of the Great Barrier Reef cannot be repaired.

I GET AN hour and a half alone in my car on the way back to the Institute, and it is enough time to listen to enough weepy music to remember that I have the urge to keep driving. Always. To keep going away, alone, without anyone who can hurt and ruin and break and die. There are cars with Christmas trees tied to the roofs, and there is a crispness that comes with a warm California winter, though there's no snow. People wear leather boots just in case. I drive.

I think of repeating the same genetic mistakes: *Run away.* My father would say: *Stay.*

Liam is half-asleep and propped up on my office door at the Institute. I nudge him gently.

"Your mom said you were on your way back here."

But I'm not ready to talk about anything like that.

"Where are the dogs?" I say.

"Tommy."

"Do you need anything from the mainland while we are here?" I ask.

LIAM HELPS ME carry a stack of books and papers to the car, and we drive to Target, where we take turns pushing a cart with a wonky wheel down slick floors and sipping Starbucks coffees. We buy in bulk: the fancy bodywash that smells like drinkable coconut, heavy-duty trash bags. And things we might not need: a new sweater and warm socks. The Christmas display shines, and beckons us to pick out an ornament, and we decide it's only fair if we each pick one. I pick a glittery bulldog, and he picks a glittery golden retriever, and we laugh because we don't have either of those dogs. We wonder if we should buy wrapping paper and bows, or if we should get Tommy the camping gear he wants, or if we should splurge on the two-for-one giant cartons of Goldfish crackers. He pulls me close to him by the pots and pans, and I'm not ready, and I'm reminded that I'm still angry, dog ornaments and all, and so he retreats and we pay for the stuff.

We load it into the truck, and we play the radio loud enough, and we weave through the traffic and back to the ferry. He stays in the car while I get out and watch Winter Island emerge from a deep breath of fog. Then we unload in unison and put things where they should be, and we dunk our hands into the small open spout of crackers and continue on. The dogs are pesky and excited, and there's no seeing past any of the fog for now.

"Is your mom coming for Christmas?" he asks.

"I think so," I say.

"What about spaghetti for dinner?" he asks.

He opens the freezer door. In my weeklong absence, he's made a lifetime supply of his famous spicy tomato sauce that we eat when we are sick, or sad, or grieving, or hungry after a day of fooling around.

"Okay."

- Long-living loggerhead sea turtles often die before they recover from trauma.
- Live long enough to fucking recover.

IT GETS COLDER, the house creaks, and Tommy and Liam wrap white lights around the tree while Rook and I argue about how many chocolate chips belong in the cookie dough. Still, I haven't begged for new rules, for all of him. My mother opens a bottle of wine and plants herself in the comfortable chair by the fire. There are presents and board games, and when Rook's parents arrive and swaddle Tommy with gifts, and us with mainland food, we are momentarily grateful. We tell our ghost stories, and someone says they miss my father. I miss my father. I miss my mother. My husband. I miss all the ghosts of our pasts.

The dogs can sleep in our bed on Christmas Eve, and Liam sleeps soundly next to me for the first time in weeks. Because it's Christmas, and because I love him, and because I want to forgive him, I let him breathe on the back of my neck in the night. In the morning, there is food, so many eggs, and my mother insists that we wear matching pajamas, and instead we wear whatever the fuck we want. We open gifts, eat more, walk around Ferry Lands and throw the ball in the fields for the dogs. No one speaks of Christ, and everyone dips their toes into the glacier-cold Pacific and then runs back to the house to find warmth.

Liam finds a boat that needs men, and it will leave in February. He says he'll finally be out of my hair. He says he can't read my mind. That he's sorry. That he doesn't know what else to say or do. If I were better at being myself, I'd say something like, *Will you meet another woman and kiss her on the mouth in another harbor, and will she call to you in your sleep and beg you to leave your wife and your life and your dogs and your pain to go back to her? Will you tell me?*

"We could use the money," I say.

Sometimes he wants to crack me open. I can tell by the desperation in his eyes during the days that are short and too-soon dark, and he wants me to just say it. Say anything. Say how hurt I am, how I'm not sure if I can move on, how I'm not sure I know how to love, if I'm sure of anything. He tries to bring it up: he tells me he loves me, he hides love notes all over the house, he does house chores, even does some of mine. We have mastered this torture.

Sometimes, I want to crack him open. To know every part of him, even the dark parts, even when he's most lonely, to understand why he loves me. To prove that I haven't fooled myself into marrying a man just like me: so eager to forget things, so eager to forgive, so eager to avoid war. I want him to tell me he knows the difference between *lonely* and *alone*. I want to know which one he is with me right now. I need him to tell me that he's sad about us, about everything that's happened, and that somehow this will make the joy even brighter. I don't want to talk about couple's cooking classes, or whose turn it is to fill up the gas cans. I want him to tell me about us.

"How about one wild night out before I go?" he says.

But I have work. And a porpoise could be born.

"You can't live like this forever," he says.

"Live like what?"

"Like it will all go away," he says.

So I agree to the night out, and I commit to lipstick, and we walk hand in hand, surrounded by silence, and then there's the winter sea and we sit down to a plate of nachos and neon-green margaritas. There are a few locals and some European tourists, and I want to ask him if he thinks it's okay to ask for a divorce in a place like this. But instead of leaving me, or me leaving him—the great fear I long for and expect—we talk about the two inches of snow on top of the volcano. And, how it feels a lot darker a lot earlier year after year. And then no one is leaving, not even me. Like he knows my plans to run, a woman from an island, who can't go anywhere, lives her life running in circles. I want to say that I hate Winter Island, that I hate myself, our life, all of the spinning, but it's not true. For a moment, he can see me, and I'm not so scared.

We stroll along the sand, and I let him do all the talking, because he's really talking. He asks if I still love him. And I say something like, *Tell me first*. And he does, and for the first time, it feels like the truth. He says sorry. Explains that until that woman, he'd never slept with anyone else; that he once saw me, years before, laughing with another man in front of Tin Pan Harbor, and instead of getting off the boat, he just got on another. And left. That maybe he's been doing this for a long time. He's tired. He wants to love me. I want to love him. So he asks if we can start over, as these new people, and he wants new rules. He promises to give me some of his pain, and I promise to give some back.

I fall onto my knees, and they plunge into the cold sand, and I drag him down with me, and I violently cry—the sounds are unknown to me, to him, to the world, and he holds me, and I let him. I guide his arms around my body and force his hands on me. Because maybe I'm good enough to let him quietly love the way he does, with missteps and all, like the harp seals must still love their young after they leave them for the wild sea. In the play version, we grow fins and roll our bodies to the water and swim together, forever.

"I'm no good at love," I say.

"Me neither," he says.

Our love is slow in the coming days, but the nights last longer, and I let him inside me. We watch old movies in bed, and laugh when the dog barks at the loud planes fluttering around the screen in *Casablanca*. My mother calls and calls, and asks if Tommy returned the too-big shoes yet or if he has had any time to play his new video game. Out the window, Tommy's running fast with a string attached to his hand, the kite like a sail in the air, and we are inside recovering with all the good spaghetti sauce before Liam must leave with the coming high tide. I wipe the bathroom mirror after a shower, and mouth to myself: *Don't go.*

Whale Fall

Carcass of a cetacean

QUESTION: What happens when something dies?

In the very beginning, when I'm showing him the island, I tell Liam I'm a mess. I tell him I don't smoke, and then I smoke a cigarette, and later a joint right in front of him, and so he does, too. In that beginning, I do most of the talking, because I fear if there is any silence, any space between, he'll leave. I tell him I have been abandoned. He says he has been left, too. I say that my father is dead. That my life isn't complicated but it isn't easy. He asks for another cigarette.

I can't remember if I was being myself, but then who else could I have been, because it all came out so fast and there was no turning back. I pretend that I am at ease, and I know I'm good at telling half-hearted jokes. I think that laying it all out—the markings on my heart—will make it easier for us later, if there will be a later. That if I say all the bad things up front, I won't have to ever say them again.

We are both silent even when I'm loud. Terrified to say things we don't want to hear ourselves. Terrified that if we say it once, everything will open up, we'll be cracked apart, and what if there is no way to seal it all back up? We say this without saying it. I say all the things that don't matter: I tell the history of the sea.

I take him to the lighthouse, because I imagine that is what a romantic person would do, but it's cold and wet there, and he slips and smacks his tailbone at the top of the stone steps. I try to help him to his feet, and he lets me, and I pull him up with my hands, and I wonder if I have ever let anyone help me. We sit on a bench on the windy bluff, and we see whales migrating south, and in my entire life on that island, I had never seen a whale from there. I want to tell him that it's a myth that it's so easy to see whales passing here, even though that's everything we tell the tourists.

He finally starts talking, about nothing and everything, about the next boat, so that I can't decide if the distant blowing of the whale matters like I thought it would.

He asks if he can hold my hand, and when our fingers lock, there's a rush, and I can't tell what's real. He tells me he wants to see me again. And again. I go home that night and cry and cry.

So we are silent for most of our first year, talking only about paint colors, future vacations. I know of his mother's broken heart, and his dad who left them for the South Seas and later, for death, and his brothers who fear the ocean. He knows of my mother, of Mary, then Tommy, and I try to tell him all about my father. But we never really say what any of it means to us. He's easy to love, because he's the kind of person who takes care of things, who doesn't tell me to quit smoking, who will just do laundry if it needs to be done. Later, he reveals that before me, he felt alone. And so it's enough for me to say I will marry him.

He's slow to tell me what he feels, but sometimes I know it when I look at the tops of his hands, because there is the regret, and the tinges of darkness. They are bruised, they are salt-crusted, they are always nicked. He won't treat them, and instead his hands are covered in bubbles of brown scabs and he just lets them heal on their own. Then little skinless white scars appear until the sun has covered them again.

I keep trying with all the talking at him, telling him the things I want, because for the first time, someone is asking. At first, it's so easy to tell him I love him. At first, it's never easy to tell him why. When he moves into my bungalow on Ferry Lands, I watch him sleep, and I make a list of the reasons I love him. And most of them are petty, but it's that for once, I feel like I am alive to feel the extraordinary weight of joy.

I'm too afraid to ask him if he feels this, too.

Before we marry, we must talk about things like what kind of car we will buy, where we will live, if we should get a dog. But it must have been mostly me talking. We decide that he will take months-long charters out to sea, because it's what he wants and knows, and we aren't sure we could do this any other way. We don't want to be alone. We say that if he meets a woman, or I find a man, it won't mean anything. It won't break us. But we promise to be loyal to us on the island, say that nothing will ruin us. At night I try to keep him awake until we are exhausted, and I ask him for a hundred ways to tell me we'll do whatever it takes to stay in love. A scab tugs on the sheet.

Before he leaves one last time before our wedding, we hike back up to the lighthouse to clean the thick lenses that protect the lamps. He reminds me of the time he slipped. He tells me he knew he already loved me then. Then the lights are brighter. Still, he tells me that when he's away, he feels gone. The distance, he says, reminds him of the distance between all things, and he fears he will push me away. I tell him I fear the same thing.

We wonder if our same fears will make us last forever. Wonder who will die first. Say, *So if we die, maybe we are not really dead.*

He tells me he'll be back again and again, and that the next time he returns, we'll get married on the beach, even if we are different people by then, even if there is rain, or something worse. He says he'll love every adaptation of me. We'll build around us.

The carcass of a whale falls slowly to the ocean floor and forms complex localized ecosystems after death. It will sustain deep-sea organisms for decades. Maybe forever. Scientists call this a whale fall.

For weeks, I have waited for blooming roses. I pick up fallen petals, the pieces that couldn't hang on. I press the skin of them between my fingers. I rub their wetness around my hand until they dissolve into nothing. The afternoons are quiet, and the sun lingers. I devote my time to my desk and watch the sea and the sky, I research how things begin and end, focus on my work, and ignore things like the post office, the mainland, and even a few of Tommy's soccer games. I wait for a full bloom until there's an early morning when the stems have likely sneezed into flickers of pink and yellow and muted blood red.

Liam finds me in the garden, pruning, tending with whatever care I have left in me. Tommy is nearby playing with the dogs, and Rook has gone again. We've spent days and weeks watching birds, and doing homework, and waiting.

Tommy rushes to Liam first, and the dogs jump from their beds and race to him, too. There is the smell in his beard of sea, of past, of love, of hate, and the edges of his hands are cracked cold with rips and scabs. I tell him I missed him.

"There are orcas out there," he says. "Might get a lot of them in the bay this year, because that water is so warm already."

On the beach, we watch for whale spouts, but it's just a long line of nothingness. All of the sea life is tucked below. Tommy runs up to the statue to sit at Francis's feet while Liam and I sit on the porch with warm coffee and cold beers, and I confess that I think Tommy and his friends smoke cigarettes up there. Liam says he's made enough money in fish to take us somewhere for the summer. I tell him a porpoise was born. He tells me the whales have scars this year. We mourn the living things to be eaten by whales and sharks. We say there is danger in warm waters.

"Did you stop in San Francisco?" I ask.

Liam looks at me. He puts his coffee and his beer on the table, and he gets into my chair, onto my lap, like a big dog, and makes me hold him. He tells me no, that I should never ask again, and he wonders if I got his letters. But I have avoided the post office, in case he didn't write, in case I couldn't deal with more hurt.

That night, Tommy and Liam fall asleep listening to my father's records. I wonder if he kissed her again, though he promised he wouldn't. And I try to explain that I love him more after this time has passed. But nothing is out loud.

• A sperm whale's lungs will not rupture under
  pressure.

I RUSH TO the post office the next day. I unlock the small PO box, and it's packed full of postcards and letters, all smashed together like a small earthquake must have shaken them into one big mass. I can't peel them apart fast enough—he's written to me on pieces of scrap paper, postcards, takeout menus. He's mailed them from cities in Mexico, and there are a thousand sorries, a thousand love letters, a thousand reasons to love him again.

There have been the times he tells me he loves me, but here is the proof that I can keep forever. I can highlight the lines and shout them at him during a fight, or sing the words to myself again and again. I try not to seep open and let it all out right there on the floor of the post office. I stuff the wad of paper into my bag.

"You hear about that storm, Evie?" an islander says.

"The warm water's up from Mexico," I say.

She points to the old television that's mounted above the head of the postal worker, who is nearly asleep behind the counter. She begs him to turn up the volume.

"It's coming fast," she says.

It's always faster than I think it will be. Suddenly, the things I couldn't have imagined are here and then over before I can blink. I look to the sky, and it's bright and clear. But the wind has picked up, the metal clasps are slamming against the flagpole, and as I make my way to the market, there's no parking, and then the warning siren has sounded. Someone near the canned food says we might see a real tornado. I'm clutching the love letters inside my bag, as if they will float away.

The checker says that they will start boarding up. The man watering the produce says he hasn't seen a storm so bad since that tsunami all those years ago. I carry the supplies to the car, and in the distance, the ferries have been halted. I catch Tommy and Liam on bikes heading west. I pull over and shout for them to get home. The rain has come. Everything happens so fast. Just everything.

"Tommy needs to board up Rook's," they say, and don't even stop.

There is something out there, and it's moving closer, and it's dark. Because the water is so warm and the air is so cold, we won't know how bad it will be. I sandbag the edges of the house, board up the lighthouse windows, prepare the flashlights and lanterns and candles. I keep the fire roaring, because it's fast, but I'm ready.

Tommy and Liam appear, and they are drenched. They help tape the windows and latch the shutters, and Tommy unplugs the things in the garage, and he spends time making the dogs comfortable.

When we eat dinner, we still have light, but the wind is rattling everything, and we eat slowly, waiting for it to arrive. Before the phones go, my mother calls, and so does Rook, and neither Tommy nor I know, really, where our mothers are.

I have thought of hiding. I have thought of running away. The thing about this island, I tell them as we sit in the great room and eat cold popcorn, is that if you live here, you are living in constant fear of never knowing. Not knowing how your life is supposed to be. Living here, I say, is to die of exposure.

The lights have gone out.

Then, we wait together. Tommy jokes that we are going to die. He falls asleep just after dinner, because of the excitement. I pull the soggy pile of mail from my bag, and I unravel Liam's love on the kitchen table. He helps drape some pages over the backs of the chairs.

When the lights go out, it's dark enough for me then. I read each letter to him with a hoisted flashlight in my hands. I read them in his voice. I make the sounds of the ocean when he writes of a storm. I cry through the parts where he tells me that he loves me no matter what.

The storm outside is louder, Tommy sleeps, still, and Liam lets me cry to him. He asks, after all these years, *Why do you love me?* I spend the rest of the night risking any escape plan, writing letters back to him instead, saying it all out loud.

Our storm feels so fast, and like it lasted forever, too. The water damage isn't so bad, because by now, we know how to wait it out, how to board it up, how to hunker down. We know what it means to be prepared. My roses are washed away, and Rook returns for Tommy—she says she feared we had all gone under—and Liam and I are wondering whether the thunderous, downpouring rains will stop, whether the humidity will ease, whether people can stay together forever.

Because now we fear the light.

- The surface layer of the ocean is the transparent one.
- The most vulnerable, too.

I HAVE NEVER known the kind of love that lasts forever. I'm always looking for a way out. I hope that, instead, someday a letter will arrive, or there will be writing in the sky, with all the answers. I say this to Liam, because he begs me to talk with words that make sounds from my lips, because as Liam always says, he cannot read my mind, and I wonder if I'm too sensitive or not sensitive enough. I wonder the same about him. He says that our betrayals don't mean we don't love one another. I ask him if we should go to counseling, and he laughs. He says he'll do anything I want to do. But

I'm still learning what I want to do. He says, *Couple's rock climbing.* I say, *Maybe.*

Some nights, I sift through his letters, because there are more stashed away in old cigar boxes and tackle boxes, from nearly a decade ago, and I wonder if it's possible to love someone with just your top layer. Or maybe Liam knows my depths, too; maybe there's just no need to speak of the darkness. He is kissing my neck from behind in the kitchen, and we are looking at the sunshine poking through moving clouds. He asks me what I'm thinking, and I am trying to figure it out. I ask him what he's thinking, and he says, *I don't know.*

"What if I'm no good at this?" I say.

I am waiting for a reply, and the dogs are barking, and I guess I don't need any answer.

We have mastered this: there are no answers. Instead of spending our hours finding the right things to say, we say nothing. This has been a joy of our marriage. This has been a wound of our marriage, too. He helps me pick up after the storm, and there are still clouds, but he sees me. He knows the ache. A lifetime of it, because he has it, too, in his own ways, and we lift torn sandbags into the back of the truck and drive around the property to assess damage. We stay busy, and the days of cleanup, the time found to work, the moments we eat at a table, I say out loud, *I am a fool,* and Liam knows. I never say I've forgiven him, and he never says he's forgiven me, but he's right there while it's all happening, right alongside everything else.

Sometimes I am going to burst. I sob into a bowl of carrot soup. I blame it all on Tommy; I say how much I miss him when Rook takes him away, that after a storm like that, I just want him close, that I'm afraid one day he'll leave the island, then I'll be alone. And Liam cries, too. He says it's Tommy, too. And suddenly, the soup is cold and we are melting together, with tears, and our constant unspoken forgiveness and anger.

- Creatures can live for a very long time in absolute darkness.
- Some glow.

I HAVE BEEN saying sorry for weeks. He has been saying sorry for weeks. The sea is calm. We pick avocados. Tommy returns for Sunday-night dinners. I think of the way it's all turning out, and of the way of all things, and how all things move.

Liam's fishing buddy lets us take out his boat to look for whales, and Rook and Tommy fall asleep in the galley just as the sun appears. There is the horizon, and there are orcas in the distance, piercing through solid sea, and our island behind us, and all that infinity ahead. I say it out loud to Liam, and he smiles, like he knew what I was thinking. There is sun on his face, and he sings a poem he wrote in one of the letters. I sing mine back.

Unbearable heat. Nothing else to talk about but the sweat on the backs of necks and the uncertainty of weather. Winter Island dreads this kind of heat, the kind that breaks people. The kind that draws people into dark caves. The kind of heat from which even after a swim, there is no relief.

Me explaining the growing of roses is me explaining that it's like the cycle of a woman—all her waiting, and watching, and sprouting, and dying. There's an exact window of time to plant a rose bush. It comes with strict rules and science, and there are miracles involved. I say this to Liam. I say my window of time is now. I'm trying to say everything.

Tommy has gone back to Rook, this time farther, somewhere in San Diego County, to a small apartment with a pool. When he calls to tell me about the pool, I can think only that life must just be longing and longing. Maybe it's my broken heart, the losing of so many things after all the years. What's really on my mind: *I may no longer be the person I once was.* But I can muster up the courage only to say, *Is it hot out there, too?*

"Unbearable," Tommy says.

The dogs have been slow. The cats, lazy. Our bodies not ready for the kind of mainland heat that has been desecrating our island. The Earth has been changing, the news tells us, and now, we are living in the extremes.

I ask myself, when Liam is away, or when he's sweaty, or asleep with his full head of hair in my lap, whether I was ever not living in a moving sea of change. And sorrow. And joy. And whether I have been living too quietly. Or too loudly. I ask myself, while touching the earth that feels like fire, whether I have been forgiving. At least to myself. When this forgiveness finally happens, *really* happens, like a pop in the brain, everything after slows down. This evolution of us is slow. It lingers. This is what I say to Liam. And things about the unbearable heat, and our unbearable love.

- It has taken 25 million years for whales to learn to be whales.
- They have enormous hearts.

I AGREE THAT an air conditioner will save us. The final thing we will need to be our real selves. To find our truest love. We get the truck serviced before we take it to the ferry, then we sit on the ledge watching for seals as we pass through the channel, before driving off into the heated and congested streets of Los Angeles, to the hardware store that sells the discounted air-conditioning units. Liam drives on the way there, and I say I'll drive on the way home. He wanders through the lighting, the plants, the sinks, the carpets, and then there are only a few air conditioners left.

"I think this one will work for the bedroom, at least," he says.

The box has been damaged, and a receipt has been taped to its side, but we don't care if it's damaged. We buy it anyway, because we are suffering, and when the checker asks if we want a bag, the joke goes unnoticed, because we are hot, and worried that our island is no longer ours. Not in this heat.

Liam says we should explore the mainland, that we don't need to be back soon, and I don't say that I have plenty of work to distract me. The truck's AC is working steady. I agree. Even in the traffic, the heat, the smog, it's nice to be cool together. Though the small of my back is sweating against my shirt and the seat, we keep driving, with the nearly broken unit fastened in the back. I keep checking out the window, at the sun, the big box, everything.

"I tied it down pretty good," he says.

The rest of the world exists outside this truck. There are so many streets, freeways, people. Sometimes, that's everything I want. We take the coast north, through the loathsome Malibu traffic, and then we wind past the county line into Oxnard, then Ventura, then past my mother's hill, all the way to Santa Barbara. Liam pumps gas, and I buy bags of bad snacks. From the gas station, we can see the rest of the Channel Islands. I point to the island where a woman was left behind, and I say her grave is nearby. I say she was dead in only a few weeks after the white men took her to the mainland and fed her things like wheat, and gave her diseases.

I don't ask where we are going, or when we will stop, and as we inch alongside the uneven edges of California, I begin to calculate how long it will take to get back, until I don't care anymore. Until the sun is not overhead and I've stopped counting the hours.

We stop at a diner, and we sit on the same side of a booth, our bare legs pressed against the seat. Our thighs meet. We acknowledge that we hate this kind of people, the kind of lovers who must always touch. We say we are not those kind of people, even when Liam feeds me bites from his fork. We share a slice of pie.

There is more driving, we trade off, and neither of us asks the other when to stop. We just keep going.

Once, Liam let me take a lick from his ice-cream cone. Knowing that his tongue had touched the ice cream first. It must have been the end of our first week. Our second date. It has been the most courageous thing I've done in my life.

We'd spent so much time together in the beginning there was a quickness to our commitment, and we holed up in the lighthouse listening for rain. He said he loved me, underneath the blankets, and even if our love were to last forever, that he'd have to eat. That we'd have to go outside, and live like people, and go get things like food and toilet paper.

I liked us standing together, him so much taller than me, everything different than me: his sandy-blond hair and broad shoulders, blue eyes, freckles and sun damage, and bad hearing. His strength from pushing and lifting and swimming and moving. I was so drawn to him, his holding my hand even if I started to let go. I worried about having a man in my things, in my home, one who wanted to stay forever.

When I met Liam, I said something terrible and dramatic, something like, *Hey, men always go to the sky or the sea.* He told me something like, *But I'm always going to be with you.* I can't remember if I told him I loved him, too, but our lives crashed together, and even when he was gone, I could feel him deep inside my bones. At first, it was so easy to be anyone we wanted to be. Then we had to learn to be ourselves. To say what we wanted. To decide what we wanted together, too.

A side-of-the-road woman asks if we want to pay the hourly rate for the room. *Sure,* we say, and Liam and I rinse off in the shower and I don't wash my hair, and we collapse on a bed together because driving is tiring. *It's so late,* we say. Running away is tiring. Evolving is exhausting. I have set an alarm to wake us in four hours, when there will be light, when we will check out of our hourly motel. We sleep tangled in the double bed closest to the air conditioner in the window. We play Twenty Questions until we're almost asleep. I ask him if he remembers the ice-cream cone, and my tongue against it, but he's already dreaming.

- Tympanic bulla: the part of the whale's ear that hears echolocation
- What if we could know when all the unbearable things were coming?

IN THE DAYLIGHT, we stop at a zoo in Northern California and stare at the hippos. There's a man with khaki pants and a khaki shirt standing on a rock, saying that this hippo, the big one he is pointing to below in a pool of water, is related to ancient whales. I roll my eyes, and Liam is proud that I know more than this khaki-colored man.

I follow Liam to the apes, and they are loud, banging on the glass, and he tells me that he wishes the animals were not in cages. He says he wishes they were free. But I explain how captivity works: They are bred into it. They cannot survive without the cage. He slumps onto a bench made of a massive slab of redwood and places his hand over his heart. He believes that they might make it on their own. Sometimes, things can overcome those kinds of pressures, he says.

We eat the zoo fast food. It's still hot, even up north. We look at a map of California.

"I should call Tommy," I say.

There is a standoff, and neither of us asks when we should go back. We keep the silence.

I have thought of other islands, the entireties of mainlands, the caverns to explore, and I tell Liam, as we keep driving, that if he wants, I'll leave Winter Island. That maybe we should try fly-fishing in Montana. That I'm ready now, to be anything with him, anywhere, and that I'm sorry it took so long. I'll need all of him from now on.

From a McDonald's parking lot, we can see the faraway kind of mountains.

"I'd live anywhere with you," I say.

He leans his head on my shoulder and dips a French fry into my ketchup, and everything smells like trees and grease. He tells me he loves me, more than anything could ever love anything, that he's sorry for hiding for so long in the light and the dark, and he checks the back to make sure the air-conditioning unit is still secure for the ride.

We have been cracked open again. Maybe for a second time, we are in love.

"I think we can make it back for the seven a.m. ferry," he says.

• Whales evolved because they had to.

MY ROSES NEED to be in the ground for a few months before the first fall frost. They must establish themselves before it gets cold. Before they go dormant. Liam and I sweat while working on the garden planters that line the house. He offers much of his time to repair what the spring storm damaged. It's the longest he's been home, and there is a list of things to fix. The porch steps, the broken windows above the garage, the bleached coral from the too-warm waters, and us. Everything, slowly, is being mended.

We talk of donating Ferry Lands to the public, or selling it to rich men, or moving to the top of a mountain, or trying to do it all underwater. But we keep moving and working and fishing and mapping and living so that we don't make any decisions with consequences. We work on our house, our flowers, ourselves, and we continue to sweat. The machine that makes the new, cool air, helps. We sleep soundly.

Liam isn't bothered when I work through the night, and he attends the fundraising events for the Sea Institute throughout the summer. He wears the same cheap suit each time, and I rotate through a series of dresses my mother has given to me over the years. He says I look beautiful, though I take off the heels on the way there and the way home. Some nights, we rent hourly motel rooms on seedy blocks in Los Angeles, and other nights, we are perfect parents and have dinner with Rook and Tommy.

It feels like there is so much change, but nothing has changed at all. I live a few blocks from the house where I was born, and some mornings, we walk by, dog leashes tied to our hands, and Liam asks me all the questions that have no answers. Some mornings, there are answers, and we talk for hours.

His fishing money lasts us for a few months. We spend most of our days locked in our bedroom, touching, working, reading, or sleeping. It's the only space that is cool enough to keep us calm. We do the rest of everything in the darkness, because it's the stillness of dark that is most comfortable. We keep the lights low, the oven off. We eat cold salads and other things from the fridge. Sometimes we suck on ice cubes. The dogs are restless, and they are panting, and they spend most of their time nestled in dirty towel piles on the bathroom floor.

• Humpbacks are nothing like their ancestors, except for their wild energy to endure.

ONE NIGHT, I tell Liam that I don't want him to go. That I want him to take only the local charters. Or to clean the bottoms of boats. That we don't need that much money. That we aren't obligated to buy Tommy backpacks and shoes anymore. That I'd eat from the garden each night and sleep under a moon if it meant he'd stay with me. I'm not sure I say it as articulately as I imagine, because I really want to say: *I'm ready now to love you forever,* even though I'd already promised that.

In the morning, he makes me say it again. Then, in the afternoon, too. He wants to hear it, again and again, until it's become a funny poem that he says when he makes scrambled eggs for dinner. Then, it becomes a song. So loud that everything can hear.

SATURDAY

My mother convinces me that we must celebrate my upcoming wedding. We must talk about womanhood with strangers or women, in bars, on this island, amid the late-night island heat. It's better than being alone with her; it's better than talking about being a woman with just my mother under fluorescent kitchen lights.

It's Creedence Night at The Wharf. The vacationers love it. There's a live band doing all the CCR covers, and the lead singer—he's from the mainland—actually looks a little like John Fogerty, but taller and more handsome. There are a lot of rough-skinned women here, all the old fake boobies, too, and we are all wearing our best. My mother has convinced me to wear her lipstick, and it's blending into a mess.

She pulls a chintzy white veil from her purse, and it's attached to a headband—the kind of thing you buy at Party

City, and she combs it right into my hair. She tells me I look beautiful. She tells me I should have worn a shorter dress to Creedence Night. We're crowding in front of the mirrors in the bathroom, and she's reapplying lipstick. She reapplies mine. Says she wishes she had lips like mine.

Other women pile in. Though it's still early, people have been drinking all day. Some came from LA just to see this fake John Fogerty. Some, just to get away. There's a woman in a mirror next to us, and she's wasted, the toppling-over kind of drunk, and she asks when I'm getting married. My mother tells her everything, and I slip out and find my way to the bar.

My mother finds me, and her new friends parade me around the room, and my mother buys shots for me. An entire group of women who are out to celebrate a recent divorce shriek with joy. We suck the small cups dry, and my whole body burns. My mother, she's on fire.

The divorced women offer us barstools at their high-top table, and my mother sits at the head. She tells stories about her divorces. She says, *Sometimes love doesn't last.* She tells them that she's happy *without anyone.* A woman chimes in with something like, *You have your beautiful daughter,* and this is when she does the thing where she pretends we are close. That I am loved. The more shots, the more doting she becomes, the more I think I am loved. It's so easy to fall for it because I want it to be real so bad.

The women follow her to the dance floor and spread out, and begin to bounce and shake. They are careful to hold their dick-strawed drinks in one hand. Careful to laugh together. To sing along with the chorus. Over the dense weight of the booming sound, they comment on her body, her swaying, in the foggy bar light; they tell her she is beautiful. A woman whispers to me that I'm lucky to have a mother like mine.

My mother holds her drink to the ceiling, and she's made eye contact with Fake John Fogerty, and he raises a beer, too, and she gets everyone to chant *Fuck divorce!*

I'm bobbing alongside my mother and these strange women and we are dancing. I'm drinking beer as fast as I can. We keep moving, and my mother wiggles her way to the front of the small crowd and sways beneath Fake John Fogerty's feet. He dedicates a song to her, and she screams to correct him, that, no, it's her beautiful daughter who is getting married, and we must toast to her. She forces my hand into the air, and there are more strangers who cheer and tug on my veil. Fake John Fogerty wishes me a lifetime of happiness from the microphone and takes a giant swig of beer.

We keep drinking. This is what I know to do. My mother ends up at another table, some divorcées follow, and one woman fans her like a real dead queen. She convinces the women to buy us more shots. We fulfill our duty and drink.

"Oh, divorces can be nasty, but they can also be the best thing that will ever happen to you," she says to one stranger.

Next there are blow-job shots. They're too sweet, and I fear the worst: I'm going to be falling-down hammered with my mother if we continue at this pace. It feels like she wants this, and with all the Creedence and the drums, I might want it, too. She's holding my hand. She's fixing my veil. She's shouting to strangers, *My daughter is getting married! My beautiful daughter! My only daughter!* And people—at least plenty of men—think we are sisters. My mother says we must keep dancing.

The Creedence Clearwater Revival cover band is getting louder. They are generous with smiles. The bar is vast, and the standing-only pit below the stage is littered with bodies, hard and soft. Like a wave, we are all moving together. My mother is eyeing this Fake John Fogerty guy, and I can't admit that I'm smitten with the drummer. He's drilling another heartbeat into my chest. We dance.

My mother is throwing her hands in the air, kicking her feet, and she's a wondrous creature. She's telling the divorced women that she once gave herself whiplash at a Van Halen show—and still managed to get backstage—and still managed to *meet* David Lee Roth. She claims that Sammy Hagar was much, much better.

I don't feel lonely when I'm with my mother. But when she's gone, I don't feel lonely, either. I can't explain it to her—that whether she's there or not, she's accidentally always with me. Even when I hate her. Even when I love her. She's just here. And now, I feel her next to me, like I do when she's gone. It's a terrifying feeling to love a woman like my mother, and all those years my father spent saying nothing about it must have been miserable. I keep drinking. I keep getting sentimental. I keep letting her hold my hand.

She's locked on to Fake John Fogerty. I slip away to the patio and smoke borrowed cigarettes with people I don't know. There are so many people stumbling in the streets, in full-vacation mode, their faces oily and burned. They are without sweaters, something they always forget, and the women are shivering, huddled together, hands cupped around the ends of cigarettes with lighters. Even heavy with the dreadful summer crowds, the island feels like home, like I am the keeper of magic here. Even on this patio, where I smoke with three practically teenage boys and they tell me they like my lipstick and my veil. They tell me they are college boys from LA. They ask me about weed.

"We're looking for Winter Wonderland," they say.

I'm drunk enough to say it: "That's my weed."

And it's all gone. I sold the name for cash to bail my father out of jail. We had to pay his debts and clean up the pieces of our lives that he ruined so long ago. I don't do weed anymore. I don't deal drugs. Now there's a company in Japan who makes a weekly cartoon called *Winter Wonderland*, with a gnome who grows magic mushrooms on a dark and stormy island near California. I hear it's a hit there. We got enough cash to pay everyone off. To keep us from being killed. *I don't know where to get it, raw and wild and organic, because it doesn't grow here anymore*, I want to say. And: *I don't have my father anymore, or a heart. I'm getting married. To a*

*man who shouldn't love me. But he does. And what if he
leaves me someday?* And: *I'm wasted.*

"You'd have better luck on the mainland," I say.

"It grows wild here, and mushrooms, too," they say.

Certainly everything is wild here, and I tell them about
the abandoned north, about the once-overgrown forest,
about the weather, about it all, until nothing makes sense.

"There were gnomes, they say, until the storms came,"
I say.

They laugh. I'm old to them. They think I'm just a
vacationer like them. They think I must have kids, a job, a
family, a life. I am all of those things and none of them at
once—looking for magic, just like them, and still looking
for my mother, who's evaporating under the bar lights. She's
talking to Fake John Fogerty on his break, and her hand is
practically on the crotch of his leather pants.

The divorced women are going to another bar, and they
beg us to come. My mother is suddenly missing somewhere
in the back, and I know what she's doing and I don't want
to know what she's doing, and I say we will meet them later.
I rush through the swinging kitchen doors and run up the
stairway to the roof.

I've been on this roof many times, before this place was
The Wharf, when my father and I ate free food from the
kitchen and lay on beach towels and did homework just for
the view. In spring, this was the place to see the great whale
migrations.

I stand on top of a rusted chair on the roof, and I stare at the sea. I look for the lighthouse. For Liam. For a boat. For a whale. For something to come into the harbor. For an answer.

"Congratulations," a man says.

The drummer. He's smoking a cigarette. He asks if I want one. I'm about to puke, and I can't decide what's right, so I take one and gag. He helps me off the chair, saying he's worried I'm a little too drunk to be on a roof, or a chair on top of a roof.

"What are you looking for?" he asks.

"I'm not sure," I say.

I'm fiddling with my veil, and it smells like smoke now.

"When's the wedding?" he asks.

"A few days," I say.

"Lucky guy," he says.

The drummer tells me about how he became a guy in a CCR cover band. He's a composer, or at least he wants to be, and he tells me about the life he wishes he had. There is sorrow in his eyes, and for a moment, he says he loves a girl who doesn't love him back, and I tell him that the man I love might be lost at sea, that my father is buried out there, too, and that my mother is probably fucking Fake John Fogerty in the bus outside.

"What a disaster," he says.

He leans in to kiss me, and for a second, I let it happen. Not because I love him, or could love him, but because of biology. See, there is biology to sex and companionship and kissing, but there is no biology to missing and loving. While his mouth meets mine, I keep my eyes open, and I look back to the sea. I talk through his attempts to kiss me, and I tell him that we must get back. That I must rescue my mother. That I must rescue myself.

My mother is not as disheveled as I'd imagined. As I'd hoped, so I could yell and scream at her and tell her she's terrible and unfair. She pulls me from the kitchen doors, and there are more shots. Someone is crying. My veil is ripped. She dances with just me in front of the band again and is twirling me around with my fingertips locked with hers. She whispers in my ear: *Don't worry, baby. Your Liam will be home.*

My mother thinks she can smell the dead whale on the ride back. We drape our arms and lean our heads outside the cab windows, and the whale is indeed still here. I puke in the kitchen sink; my mother, in the bathroom. We sleep on the couches that face each other, our arms curled under our chins in the same exact way.

Hail

It came at night, sometimes without any rain or warning. A sudden chill and then the pounding of ice that sounded like sand dumped on the roof. It came with force, and it just kept coming. Rook sat in her hot tub as ice fell from the sky, piercing the tops of our heads. We were hot on the bottom and cold on top.

The winter that Rook got a hot tub was the winter lived in water. The hot tub was sturdy, on a deck in her enormous backyard that overlooked the Pacific Ocean. She loved to tell people about her house, designed by her famous architect father; he'd imported the tiles from around the world. Rook's stepmother designed their estate gardens after Versailles. The cacophonous hail on that roof was a musical every time.

Her mother hated the hot tub and regretted allowing the eyesore on her property. Hot tubs were for the trashy kind of people. And horny teens. But for the first time in her life, Rook got an A, and she was allowed one gift—anything she wanted. Of course she wanted a hot tub, one with all the fancy jets and bucket seats and neon sex lights. Of course Rook wanted to smoke cigarettes and be touched by guys from the beach in that tub with intermittent hailstorms swirling overhead.

Her parents tucked it behind tall trees and concealed a giant tub of water behind lattice walls of night-blooming jasmine. Maybe they didn't care that Rook was having sex, or maybe they did, but they surely let it happen all the time.

We lived as prunes for an entire winter. We bought bags of sour candy and packs of Camels and soaked in bubbled scalding water until we couldn't take it anymore. Until the hail made us bleed. For hours, we'd listen to Snoop Dogg and talk about how fun it was to show our tits to strangers. There were hours of stupid existential conversations. We said we wanted to be wild, but I never meant it the way she did. We promised to love each other forever, no matter what.

"My cousin said he can get us into a show in LA," she said.

"My dad would never let me go to the mainland for that," I said.

"Don't tell him," she said.

We planned it for weeks, and I told Dad that I'd stay at Rook's for the weekend. She knew a guy with a boat that could get us to the mainland without taking the ferry, without being spotted, without the weather shutting things down. Her cousin would pick us up at the harbor, and we'd stay with him for a few nights. Easy.

Dad and I had a burger at our favorite spot. We talked about Rook's new hot tub, the recent flurry of garibaldi, the flurries in the sky, whether or not everyone eventually gets chicken pox. It was seamless. He was drunk when he dropped me off. He didn't know her parents had been in France for three weeks.

"Don't piss her parents off and sneak out," he said.

Rook popped out, bikini only, and waved to Dad.

We drank champagne and danced sopping wet to music videos on the TV. Clinked our glasses together and sat in the hot tub until the sky raged. We dressed up, and we recorded our own music video. When we were coming down and exhausted, she said we could go to the mainland in the late afternoon the next day. She was finally eighteen, and joked that she'd take care of us if anything happened.

"I'm glad we're friends," I said.

"Forever," she said.

We sat close on the couch. I thought of all the people who have been left behind, about the lonely people my father warned me about. I adored Rook's nose, because it was perfect. I admired her capacity to be able to shove all her emotions into some small box hidden in her body, until she was cool and clear and calm all the time. I was reeling. And wondering. And waiting.

Half-asleep, she asked me if I'd ever been left behind. *Sometimes*, I thought but couldn't say. I couldn't tell her because there were more pressing things, like: I had never had good sex. What if my father left me too? What if I never found love? What kind of cheese did I like best?

"You should really sleep with an older man," she said then. "They treat you good."

"I need dry clothes and bed," I said.

I followed her down all the halls and into the bathroom with all the mirrors.

I SENSED THAT Rook had left me behind. While she was standing in the tub and shaving her legs and bikini line and arms, I had rifled through her vanity, spraying all her perfumes, and found a pair of my father's socks, with the hole in the right toe, and I knew she had decided to abandon me for him. Also: a birthday card for her written in his handwriting, signed, *Love you always*. Maybe I knew it before, but I'd been so good at believing bad things weren't so bad.

I remembered that once, I'd come home from school, and Rook was already there. She was in tiny shorts, sprawled out on the couch so that Dad could practically see her labia. Conveniently, she was at my house a lot. When I wasn't there. Dropping in to see Dad. Sometimes, Dad would put on Dusty Springfield and cook dinner for us. He'd say that we were his *favorite girls*. I'd hated Rook for the way she pined over him, but told myself her pain was deep, so was mine, and that things could be fine, that she didn't mean it the way it seemed. I'd hated Dad for this, too, but made myself believe that they both needed this crush. And I was quiet.

Until the holed-sock in her drawer. I told her I hated her, and I threw Rook's parents' fancy champagne onto the bathroom floor, and the mirrors reflected an infinite version of all the glass. Threw the borrowed sweatpants at her, grabbed my things, and left.

She chased after me, crying. She yelled that she'd stop if it bothered me. She said that despite everything, she was in love with him, and she didn't know what to do. Then she sat on the front porch of her lighted mansion and said if I left her, she'd have nothing. That he'd never choose her over me. She said no one would love her like I do.

Even when I hated her, I believed it, too. I couldn't abandon her, because then I'd be a person who could leave anyone. She said she'd stop. The hail played a song on the roof, and I couldn't turn back.

I DIDN'T GO home. Everything was a haze. The sky was up and down, and nothing felt real. An island is round. Even if it's oblong, it's round, made of one continuous line that never ends. There's nowhere to go. Except up into the sky, or underwater, but still, it will always feel like you're spinning. I rode my bike around until very late, until I was very cold and hail-beaten. The uncomfortable parts of my bathing suit were still damp. I slept in the topiary garden at Ferry Lands, and the hail turned into drizzle, and then nothing at all.

In the morning, I awoke to a gardener poking me with the end of a rake. I told him I was just visiting Mary, and that I was on my way out. I picked a few oranges and sat on the beach, sucking the life out of the fruit and trying to remember that thing people always said: *Things will get better.* Dad always said: *It's just what happens.*

I said I was sick and locked myself in my room. Dad left soup at the door. Rook never went to the mainland to see the show and her druggie cousin. Instead, she lingered around my house until I finally came out, and she held me close, and told me she was the sorriest. She blamed her life. Her eyes ballooned, and I guess we were friends again. Because the worst part was that I loved her. She promised that it was only once, and that she'd stop, and that we'd never tell anyone. I didn't forgive her, but I said that I would try.

At night, alone on the couch, I listened to the hail tap on windowpanes, and I cried. I cried and cried. I pretended to be fine, to Rook, and to my father. No one taught me what to do with my mad.

And I didn't speak to my father until I finally did.

"Where is my mother?" I asked my father.

He was shaken by my curiosity.

"I haven't heard," he said.

He opened a cheap bottle of vodka.

"Can I have some?" I said.

"Fuck, no, you cannot have any vodka," he said.

I slammed the front door as I walked out and scurried down the stairs. That betrayal hard as a rock.

My father shouted from the window something about how I needed to be home for dinner. He used his *discipline* voice. I told him to fuck off, in my loudest, most protesty voice, and I guess he thought it was hormones, because when I got back for dinner, he had two bars of chocolate on the coffee table.

I didn't tell him that I knew, because I didn't want to be the one to kill him. So we spoke only about the things required, and I let him believe it was because I was a teenager. Like homework, staying out too late, dinner. When he brought up Rook, I played along, like he was just concerned about her reckless life and missing parents.

But he knew I was different, and I wondered if Rook had told him or if she must have really backed off. And the silence was easier than asking for the truth, and there was more booze then, more nights he didn't come home, more coke binges, and I didn't care for a while if he was dead.

On nights he escaped, I did, too, and I rode past Rook's to see if he had gone there. I never caught them, if they were a *them*. I didn't want to. I just saw Rook alone in her hot tub, talking to herself, as if she were being interviewed on a talk show. Or Rook drunk in her hot tub with a few girls we swore we hated from school. Or Rook alone in the darkness, alive only by the light of a movie on a screen, and then more nighttime.

There are so many things I never said, because how can you say all the things when no one is ever listening? What I should have said, loudly: *I really hate hot tubs. I hate everything about them. That hot water feels like it is penetrating my heart. It makes it skip beats, my skin goes red for hours, I can't sleep, I feel so hot, and with the hail, it's worse, and confusing. A tiny pool of murky water is not my idea of a good time. Also, I bet there were traces of cum all over that fucking hot tub.* Also: *How could you do this to me?*

Rook told me about a guy named Sam, who knew that Bunny was dating some rich summer girl. Sam said they were falling in love. Rook said that if I wanted, she could break up Bunny from his girl. She told me that Bunny fucked this girl on the empty lifeguard tower just last week. Rook told me that I should just get over Bunny, and meet someone new, like she'd done.

I didn't say anything about my father, because the days and weeks that had passed were somehow erased from our lives. Because I was so good at participating in that kind of forgiveness, the kind that meant only to be forgetful.

I told her I was not ready to give up on Bunny, that I thought I loved Bunny, and she told me to shut the fuck up, and to calm the fuck down, and to chill the fuck out.

"Let's go to the hot tub," she said. "I'll tell Sam to bring a hot friend."

"The hot tub is too hot," I said.

She laughed, and told me I was the most *wicked funny* person she knew. I tried not to hate her. I wanted to tell her that I worried about weather, my father's dental bills, climate change, the sea—*oh, everything in it, even the bad, dark stuff*—worried that I was a bad kisser, that my breasts were crooked, my nostrils too big, about my mother, smog, and that I never, ever knew where I should be going, even in the light, that I knew she never really meant *forever*. But mostly, I wanted to tell her that I really hated hot tubs. That drinking vodka in there made it worse.

We slid in, and she turned the lights to flashing purple.

"Do you think it's bad that we don't have any other friends?" I asked her.

"We do," she said.

"Who?"

She named, then, girls (mostly) from school who we shared cigarettes with after class, or who she got hammered with at parties; she even named the school janitor, who if you asked me, she really liked and had probably kissed at least once.

"And your dad. He's a cool guy, and a good friend."

I shriveled. We smoked more.

I'd imagined my father passed out on the bathroom floor, where he'd been trying to clean up his own mess.

"Do you believe in ghosts?" she asked.

"Never," I said.

But I had known so many ghosts.

"I can show you one."

THEN MORE BUD, more vodka, and us drying quick in the cold wind and us squeezing our damp bodies into cool clothes. She was so comfortable being topless, with her perfect nipples. She must have known she flaunted them to me, or to the staring-back sea, or to the moon.

We rode our bikes, with all that wet hair, and pedaled and huffed nicotine, and then more hail came. I didn't ask where we were going, because anywhere was better than going home. Even if it meant going someplace with her.

Down a dark road was a house with a koi pond. Rook leaned her bike against the bamboo fence. She urged me to be quiet, to leave my bike behind. She pointed to an upstairs dimly lighted room. I told her I didn't see anything. She told me to wait, and we kept walking. I followed her to the house, through the unlocked gate, into the garden. She promised ghosts.

"All you're promising is to get me arrested," I said.

The yard was only a concrete wall from the bay, and there were leftover wakes slapping lightly against it. The grass was cold and wet, and it soaked our shirts when we lay down. She talked softly, and everything was so dark, and she had a granola bar in her pocket. We split it and sipped the plastic bottle of vodka. We were mostly warm, even with the pricks of ice that dented our faces. That yard was magnificent.

"This is where I come for shooting stars," she said.

"It's too foggy," I said.

For a minute, I forgot about the ghost and snuggled next to her.

"Stay awake," she said. "A dead old lady is going to walk by the window."

She quietly sang to me, and I felt loved and whole, even with all that betrayal. Then, I couldn't keep my eyes open for any ghost anymore.

EVENTUALLY, I WENT home to my father. I helped him sober up again. I got him a job on a boat, and he'd be gone for a few months. I told him to come back with money. He told me to tend to our weed. We didn't talk about our spinning web of tiny betrayals. He'd return, and I expected that I'd tell him that I loved him, and then I would probably eat lobster for dinner for an entire week.

Before he went, he looked up to me and said, from the small, decrepit balcony, "I think the hail has finally stopped."

"Do you believe in ghosts?" I asked.

Wind

The wind swept through Ferry Lands and whipped up the dusty hills and sank dirt into all the cracks. Even Mary complained. Mary was no biological mother, but she had motherly things: string cheese, apples in a large bowl, warm blankets, a patio full of wind chimes. In the crevices of her house were tumbleweeds of dust, and doors ridden with dampness, and the whole thing smelled like an old boat. A favorite smell. Her house creaked in the night, and its aching bones wobbled in the tug of a storm. She kept a fire most nights, and I spotted her sliver of a smoke trail like the North Star.

The girls in high school called her a witch and a dyke. But I believed Dad used to love her wholly, by the condition of her seasoned hands, by the hours she'd logged at sea, by the sight of her holy long hair. I knew that she could fix an open wound with superglue. Once, a girl called her an *old lesbian*, and it was Rook who punched that girl in the face. *No one talks about your Mary,* she'd said. And it was true that I wished Mary was my mother, especially when I couldn't find my own.

Dad joked that we could never go to the mainland, because then we'd have to get on Mary's ferry. He said she had a temper, and that if she had the chance to, she'd sink that fucking thing and run my father's face into the muddy bottom of the bay. Her marriage didn't work out, and the distance between her and my father grew, even after he told her again that he loved her, so I had to keep Mary a secret. I told my father that I wouldn't take the ferry, because of Mary and a list of other semitearful things, that I'd have to stay on Winter Island forever. But it wasn't true, and when he was away, I'd ride the ferry at night with Mary and sit in her booth, and sometimes we had covered so much open water that I finally got sea legs. I'd tell her about Dad and all his weed money, about school, about Rook, and she listened to all the things I wanted.

There were cold nights when Dad stayed late in the fields and spent long hours organizing a small army of men who would carry military-sized rifles and protect electric fences that fortified his massive weed grow. My father and I were in the business of surviving betrayal; we were kind, but we spent as many hours apart as possible. Maybe he knew that I knew, but Rook moved on quickly to a guy our age, and my father invested all of his time into growing Wonderland. I spent nights alone, waiting for Rook to sneak boys into my bedroom, reading romance novels, or writing letters to my mother that I tossed out after a few lines of bullshit and begging. In that winter's one-bedroom apartment, Dad slept on the couch and I got the bedroom, and I might as well have just lived alone. I waited for the sound of the ferry horn coming into the harbor.

I often sneaked onto Ferry Lands the back way so that the automatic lights wouldn't shine. I'd sit quietly on Mary's vast lawn and watch the sea turn purple by the light of the moon. Some nights, I crept onto her porch and rocked in her chair and basked in aching. Sometimes, I could feel the warmth seeping from cracks in her house. Other nights, I actually peered into her windows, hoping to be caught, and fed, and loved, and understood. I tried to stay away from her, and that house, to be loyal to Dad, but when the winds blew, her garden snowed with white flecks of jasmine petals.

Then some nights, there were wool blankets left out to dry out in the sun and mistakenly left behind by nightfall. I wrapped myself in their thickness, her scent, and the leftover dog hairs. On the darkest night, there was an eyelash left of moon, no wind, no sound, the lighthouse quiet and dark. She must have heard me roaming through the fields of citrus, cracking dry things under my feet, inching my way along the dusty trails that led to her door. That dark night, Mary sat on the porch and waited with the dull glow of a lantern.

"Power's gone out on the whole island," she said.

I paused.

"I'm just glad it's been you," she said. "There are coyotes that come for the dogs."

She said she'd wondered who, over the years, had crawled about looking for shelter on the emptiness of this land, where people came to fuck and kiss and fight. Where the dogs came to die. The others to eat. She said she'd wondered how many had lived in the divots of this land, and how many she'll just never know existed.

The dogs rallied around my feet and jumped and made high-pitched screeches with their breaths. We sat in two chairs close to the fire, and it took a lot of our stillness to keep the dogs calm. When it was late, after we had said all of the useless things, she wrapped me in a blanket and brought me a cold piece of apple pie on a paper plate.

I finally told her about Rook and my father, and she didn't say anything, except she stroked my hair, and that was too much. She told me about the mainlanders who wanted to build a bridge. The clocks flashed, and there was a short flicker of electric light. She said the winds were too rough to get back to my father, that I'd have to sleep there and be gone before dawn so my father wouldn't worry. She opened a chest and pulled out two pillows. As she shook off dust, she said the only guests she gets *are raccoons*. She pulled out a book, a blanket, and a flashlight, and I climbed onto the couch.

"I've got an early morning," she said.

I fell asleep fast, next to her fire, Mary and the gaggle of dogs asleep in the bedroom.

In the morning, the power was back, and she had made coffee and left *The Origins of the Earth and More* with a note that said: *Return the book if you find what you're looking for.*

ONCE, I FOUND my mother in the innards of the dusty San Bernardino Mountains. She was a waitress in a seedy mountain bar and grill, which was mostly a bar, and I was finally old enough to drink. It was messily overgrown with bikers, and they served fries with A.1. Steak Sauce. The chef, also the owner and my mother's boyfriend, made garlic fries on Wednesdays. I took the ferry, a bus, a train, and a taxi, and if I could have, I would have latched on to a flightless bird if it had promised to get me there faster.

My mother was surprised that I found her. She acted happy, like a good mother, but talked so much at first that she wasn't listening to anything I said. She said she hated Winter Island. She said she always felt trapped. And while she was wiping down tables with a damp rag, she told me she was sorry for leaving. Though it had been years, my mother was just like I remembered her: indifferent and aloof and always looking to the sky.

"Did your father tell you where I was?" she asked.

I said that I found her on the internet. That her blog, *Mountain Mama*, came up if you searched her name. I'd

seen her daily mundane adventures in gardening and growing her own vegetables. Her photos were crooked with poor
resolution, and her blogs were boring and sometimes full of
typos. The garden seemed to make her happy, and I wondered if that is the way for women to be happy, with straw
hats, cutoff denim shorts, tan stick legs, and lemonade on
a porch swing. On the internet, my mother looked like a
wonderful mother.

"Is your father sick?" she asked.

"He's fine," I said.

I wanted to ask why she left, but she would just say she
could never stay. I wanted her to look into my eyes to see
if she could hold a gaze for long enough to see that they've
changed color with all the hurt and exhaustion. I wondered
if our eyes were the exact same color. I followed her to each
table while she wiped with vigor and stamina, and she asked
me to help fill napkin dispensers and grimy glass ketchup
bottles.

"Lunch rush gets real busy up here," she said.

My mother's arms were mine. Her hair, too. Her skin
hung a little farther from the bone. Still, she was fit and covered in a spritz of perfectly appointed freckles, and she was
firm around her rib cage, which protects her middle things.
Two bikers called to her, and she wedged herself between
them at the bar while they talked to her as if she were the
most wonderful woman ever.

"You gotta meet my daughter," she said.

She introduced me like I was no secret. Like she had told people about this daughter. One who has lived and breathed elsewhere. She called me a daddy's girl. She wouldn't say if she left me or if I left her, but it didn't matter, because she told everyone how pretty I was, and how proud she was to be a mother to me. Me.

My mother mixed drinks behind the bar, and she tossed me a key to her place, which was just up the hill and behind the restaurant parking lot. Told me to go there until she got off, if I wanted, she said. She asked me to stay for dinner, at least. She must have known that I needed her, or the idea of her, even for just one night.

"You look like a grown woman," she said.

She stared.

"Beautiful," she said.

My mother's house looked just like the photos—mismatched watercolors framed in thrift-store wood, signed by her, hung all over the walls. She had an easel on the patio, a small fire pit, because she's always loved to watch things burn, and then a wild garden—in raised boxes, in the ground, and in handmade plastic-and-PVC greenhouses. It was all unkempt.

I opened the kitchen drawers and bathroom cupboards, and sifted through her closet. She loved paisley print, Leonard Cohen, white tea, black tea, herbal tea, cheap hairspray, and that hippie kind of toothpaste. She had a storage closet full of workout balls and light weights, yoga mats, and those long, stretchy wire things that do something to sculpt muscles. I snooped so much that I was the real kind of tired, and I read whatever I could find on her bookshelf, until I fell asleep in a low-hanging hammock out back.

She woke me with a chilled hand on my cheek.

"There are lots of bugs out here," she said.

My mother prepared dinner and assigned me the small kitchen tasks, like cutting tomatoes and cucumbers for salad and, then, peeling potatoes. She was the kind of person who was always alive, and especially in her kitchen, she had a face full of color. She did the talking—about her garden, her paintings, her art shows, the time she almost made it as a painter and poet in San Francisco or Seattle. She called me by my real name, and it was not even my name anymore—Evangeline—so it sounded like she was talking to a stranger. I hated her and still missed her, too.

I asked her why I am Evangeline, for whom I must be named, and she says she just liked the sound, that I'm the first one she knew, and I was limp with disappointment that I was just a regular person. She sang my name and smiled.

Her patio overlooked the slope of backyard, and I swatted bugs from my neck while we ate. The bug zapper kept electrocuting invisible alive things, and I kept flinching. She talked over the death sound, more eager to tell me about her, until a tall man appeared in the doorway, and I recognized him from the bar, the blog, the photos on the refrigerator.

"The famous Evangeline," he said.

So I smiled, because there's nothing she could have done or said that would have made anything better, and I told myself there were no answers.

They told me about their life together. It was a whole life. And no one asked about my life, my almost-whole life. They talked into the night, even when they drove me down the hill to an empty bus stop, and they told me to come back soon. Against a settled sun and an early purple sky, I headed west. I could have evaporated before I got back to the sea, and at red lights before the freeway, I admired the fresh apples and avocados that rolled around in the bag on my lap.

Sperm Whale

Physeter macrocephalus

QUESTION: Is a sperm whale vengeful?

When your father lies to you, it will be the wave you've turned your back on. The one that hits you so hard that you scrape your knees on the ocean floor. The kind of wave that makes your knees bleed for a week. The kind of knees that must be attended to by tweezers, antiseptics, gauze, and tape. That kind of lie is the one that will scar your limbs and make you wonder if you'll ever turn your back to the sea again.

But it's the first rule of the ocean. Never, ever turn your back to the sea. She will get you. She will roar. She will teach you a lesson. It's in the way your father always nodded—*dontturnyourmotherfuckingback*—when he let you swim alone when you were small, without fins, without floaties, without anything but your skin and your suit.

When your father becomes so desperate and lonely, isolated by every passageway of water, he'll do terrible things. He will lie and tell you that he's got cancer. That the doctor told him so. He will have said things like that before—separated shoulder, thrown-out back, gallstones, kidney failure, and more—because he needed you, or money, or affection, or consoling. But he'll never say *cancer* until you are good and gone and barely coming back to the island. *Cancer* is the wave that knocks you right out of your suit, out of your skin, smashes you to the ground, and holds you down with such force that you can't find up.

Your father will tell you that this time—yes, really, this time—he is telling the truth. That he didn't want to worry you while you were away, and that now he must tell you, because it might be serious. You'll tell him that you'll come home—the next ferry out—that your small fellowship at the Institute isn't that big anyway, that you'll leave your boyfriend (you don't really love him) and you'll put him back together again. And then he'll say, *No.* He'll say, *Absolutely not.* He'll say, *Just wire me five thousand dollars.*

Then you'll know that wave is crashing right on top of you.

You will sit, crying, on your bathroom tile floor, uncomfortably leaning against the hard rim of the tub. He'll be on the other line, crying, too. But you'll know he's crying only because his desperation has taken hold; he hates asking you for things. He'd rather charm an entire island out of their money, their panties, their homes, before asking you for anything. But he will ask this one time. He'll say cancer is *fuckingexpensive.* Say that with the money, he can make rent, pay his hospital fees, and make it out—just as good as new. Because that's what the *fuckingexpensive* doctor tells him.

When your Dad is an addict, he can still be a good man. He can also be a bad man. When he's using, he'll simply be both. On the phone, you'll hear the bad man talking, the desperate one who needs love and money, and you'll still hear the good one, too. His tears won't be for the fake cancer, but for humiliation.

You will find your mother again in the dusty mountains, to ask her a favor. You'll explain to her, over the best garden salad you've ever had, that your father is still a drunk, and he pops pills, and he uses whatever he can party with, and that he's always broke. Even though he sells weed, even though he rips off the tourists, even though he's owned boats. He's never got enough, because there's never enough money to feed a man like that. You'll tell her softly, so she can try to understand, because your charming father taught you to talk that way. She'll smile sweetly, like maybe she knows you, and hand you an envelope of cash that she keeps hidden under a floorboard in the garden shed.

She will touch your face, and for once, she's not a stranger.

"Least I can do," she'll say.

For a moment, you'll think now would be the time to tell her what she can actually do. She can come around; she can fix him. Though you know she can't, that's how it's supposed to work, until she tells you no one can fix him. That that kind of love is not fixable. It's just there—take it or leave it, good and bad.

You'll know you can't say much more to her and risk her taking the money back. You'll smile sweetly, like he taught you, and you'll tell her you want to see her more, even if you really don't.

It's the least you can do.

When you overnight a UPS box of cash—from the weed, from your mother, from your friends, and from your night job in the cafeteria—you won't hear from him. You'll text over and over again. You'll get nothing back. That wave has smashed you so hard, and now you're sitting alone, with empty pockets, and looking at your own home from the other side of the water. It doesn't matter where the money went, you'll think. You just know he must have needed it more than you. That's what your mother said; that's what you keep telling yourself.

He will avoid you for as long as he can, and finally, a few months later, you've kept calling and you'll catch him in the lobby of Otto House, and you'll have the front-desk girl put him on the phone. He'll think it's a hotel guest. He'll think they need him to make them laugh. He'll think it's to sell weed.

His voice will drop, and yours will raise. How can you hold back the tears?

You won't believe it. The treatment is working, he'll say.

So you're all right, then? you'll ask.

Better than ever.

It will feel like drowning, except worse, because no one actually drowns.

Freeze

Once, my mother appeared with hair streaked blond and bright meticulously colored-in pink lips. She said she was sorry it had been so long but blamed me for not getting the letters she'd sent to an old address. She said that when she didn't hear back, she thought she'd come check on her *baby*. She couldn't stop saying how cold it was. I told her it was a freeze, and that we were all freezing.

All of that at the doorstep made my father and me uncomfortable, and still, I let her in, and she plopped onto the couch and asked for a vodka ice.

She rambled on about her new project at the Sea Institute. She said it happened by chance; my mother was seating tables in Santa Monica when she befriended a regular, a research fellow who focused on the mating rituals of porpoises, and—just like that—the PhD was impressed with my mother's intricate knowledge of land and sea. My mother said she wasn't, *like, a research person, or anything*, but she helped organize files, and made spreadsheets with porpoise-mating-ritual numbers.

"Oh, it's your dream," she said to me.

I tried to conceal that I rarely dreamed—that each night I slept soundly, either stoned or buzzed, or exhausted from sorrow, or tired from thinking of boys and television and trees and snakes and monsters. I knew that dreams were just dreams and that nothing really came true, especially if you wanted it to.

She handed me a folder, and when I opened it there were applications and forms, and signatures highlighted in yellow. She said I could work as a research assistant with this PhD person, who would help me get into the Institute program someday, or work in the oceans, or do whatever it was I had always wanted to do with all those things that lurked in the depths below.

"You could at least try it out," she says. "You can stay with me."

My father paced and paced himself right outside the door for more beer. My mother wanted to take me to dinner. Everything was so loud, and my mother, she just kept talking. About the tanks filled with sea life, about the people saving the oceans, about the cafeteria, about the little bungalow she had on the border of Venice, about how her life was somehow all put back together again, and how she really loved me. And that it was time I tried being a woman with a real woman around. Said I needed mothering. Said it was time for guidance outside of the sea and the sky.

The worst part was, I really didn't want to say no, so I said nothing, as some sort of secret compliance. Before my father returned, red-faced, and after my mother caught the last ferry back, I lay on the carpet and scratched my back the way I did, so hard, when I had chicken pox in kindergarten. The itch, though, it just didn't go away.

Why do you want to work for The Sea Institute? Please explain in a paragraph or less.

(We call them by different names, but these waters are one. Still, we have categorized five major oceans: Pacific, Atlantic, Indian, Southern, and Arctic. It would take fourteen years to sail these waters. Dad says someday we will do it. All 361.9 million square kilometers left to explore. But he never leaves. Also, we saw *Titanic* seven times in the theater. My tears were endless; my love is still boundless. Deep as that sunken ship and as dreamy as a frozen Jack crusted and attached to a limber piece of wood. Also, if I don't go now, who will be left to bury me here?)

IT'S TRUE THAT my father drank to celebrate. When he was sad. When he was unsure. When he was hurting. When he was hoping. When I told him that I was moving to the mainland with my mother. Just for a year, I promised, and I hopeful-joked that even if it was terrible, I'd have to go find out for myself. My father drank himself to sleep for a few weeks. Rook cried. Mary told me I'd always have a place at Ferry Lands, and she told me to write.

I never told anyone that I just wanted my mother to *get* me, just once, just for a year, just us watching dolphins swim in see-through-walled aquariums. Because how do you ask someone to see you?

My mother secured a two-bedroom apartment near the Sea Institute and an extra bike that I could ride to work.

"What do you like to eat?" she asked.

"I'll eat anything."

"Can you cook?" she asked.

"I think so."

My stomach was in knots for a week before I left, and I chased Rook around Winter Island. We camped in the old bat caves near Ferry Lands, and we made out with tourists and smoked spliffs. We lay atop grasses and gazed up to the sun until we were almost blind, and even then, when her fingers were interlaced in mine, she told me again and again how much she loved me and how sorry she was.

"I have a tattoo guy on the Venice Boardwalk," she said. "I'll probably come out a lot to finish this sunset on my back."

We held hands at the going-away party Dad threw at Rocky's Fish N Chips. It was a full day of adults getting blitzed and then a wild roundup of men who took us on boats to fish for whatever we could find. Dad put his arm around me, and pulled me close, and whispered that I could come home, even if this wasn't a real home, anytime. That day, he puked over the side of the boat and, somehow, my legs and stomach were sturdy. Rook kissed an older man who could crush Coors cans and wore a found captain's hat.

The remaining days before I really left were busy with Dad keeping a steady buzz and organizing and reorganizing our things to make the house appear tidy. He made dinner with fancy sausages and steaks, and let me sip red wine. We watched every sunset, and sometimes, it felt like we were dying. We spent an afternoon at the abandoned Institute and traipsed along pungent cannabis fields that flickered green against wet soil and a backdrop of massive trees. I smoked joints and ate grilled-cheese sandwiches, and the wind whipped hair all over my face. Sometimes, Rook was there, too, like I was terminal, like I was never coming back. We spent the last mornings dunking our hands into water-filled coral holes at the tide pools. We saw Old Tropez's headstone.

The sun was inching away from us on my last night. My things were packed. My father had been out all day, fishing and working, he said, and we would meet for one last cheeseburger in town. It was scratched onto our wall calendar in pencil. But he never showed.

WE USED TO say that everything was broken most of the time: the fish tank with a slow leak; the fish, a Carnie Wilson and a Joe Montana, who died on the laminate of a living room floor. A homemade lava lamp without lava—a watery grave of a lamp with an occasional glitter fleck floating around. Still, I plugged it in and used it to illuminate one of our dining room tables. The Barbie Dreamhouse, drunkenly put together backward. All of my Kens sitting on bowlegged chairs and doors opening from the outside in. A collection of lost-and-found items from Otto House, which included holey rain jackets, twisted umbrellas, too-small shoes, and vacation hats smelling of body odor and astringent. All the trash bags had rips. The carpets were never clean.

My father bought an always-broken pickup truck from a neighbor. He'd promised a year's supply of Winter Wonderland in exchange for a beat-up piece of scratched red metal. At first, she hummed. We cruised the streets with the windows down and our arms slung around her sides. Even in the rain. We installed a new radio, and my father turned up the volume at red lights. My father honked at Rocky's Fish N Chips and revved at bouncy bikini boobs roller-skating in front of Otto House. He waxed the damn thing every day. He parked her in our gravel driveway, which was so slim that we had to pull the mirrors in tight. Her wretched, rusted squeals sounded like whales passing in the night.

My father called the truck Maybellene. Must have been the red on that truck that inspired all the Chuck Berry on the stereo. Our first car was incapable of just working, or being easy or reliable. My father's Maybellene suffered from heat exhaustion, from screaming brakes, from problems with the starter, among all the other things.

We cruised on Sundays, during the lull of the season, the hunkering down in the cold. We were heading uphill the day Maybellene broke down; she just suddenly sighed and stopped altogether. I enjoyed the hill view of perfect sunset, but we had to leave her and walk home to call for help. He kicked her hard, until his feet must have bruised her tires. Until he must have broken his toes.

"Godfuckingdamnthisgoddamnplace," he yelled.

Rain the whole walk home.

We ate dinner under an awning outside 7-Eleven: warm-spun hot dogs from the case, and chips. Our favorite, anyway. My father let me have a Coke. When he was that angry, my father drank tea. Because there wasn't enough booze to calm him. He sipped it slowly and took deep breaths.

I arrived the next day on foot, and Maybellene was coned off by the Winter Island Police. Traffic swelled up just to pass her, tourists cursing our slow-moving task handlers. My father carried a few tools and a gallon of water. I sat on the curb and watched the Sea Institute vans piling off the island. Full of young and eager faces that I imagined to have waterproof bags full of sea treasures.

When her engine started, my father shouted for me to jump into the moving truck. He said she couldn't stop until we got home. He played Chuck Berry again, and the sound rattled against her metal shell. He told me to steer for him while he opened a can of Coors. I steered the whole way home, my face an infinite smile.

He washed her that night, and he washed her even when the mainland was full of drought and we were sharing water. Even when it rained. Especially when it rained, and even when everything else was broken. Among the sea of things he could not do, there were some things he certainly did well. Not everything was broken.

I WAITED FOR an hour. I knew he couldn't do it, like he couldn't do a lot of things, but I continued to sit on a wobbly bench outside the burger place until I ordered and ate alone. I tried to compartmentalize all of our little tragedies on Winter Island. I tried to focus on the onion and lettuce and meat, but I was just chewing over gulps of anger and tears. I told myself that, though he was flawed, he loved me, and as I drowned in Diet Coke, I wondered if it was enough. The restaurant began to fill with the Saturday night crowd, and I rushed out, sauce all over my face, to avoid saying any more goodbyes. It was especially cold, and I wished I'd brought my jacket for my ride home.

My father always said not to look for him. But I rode slowly, peering into the yellow light of every bar on my way home. I told myself so many things: he was home, he was asleep, he was sorry, he was busy saving a dolphin tangled in a fishing line, he loved me, he really, really did. But in the dim glow of a bar window, he was sipping a beer, with a few men around him roaring with laughter. I thought of marching in there, of scratching his face off, of really getting loud and telling him how terrible he was, but there was a worse problem: I wasn't sure I felt that way.

He was using his hands to tell a story. More laughter. His face was red. Maybe he was talking about me. I sat on the seawall, close enough to him that if I yelled he might have heard me, and watched fog turn the streetlight orange. I smoked a cigarette that Rook had stashed in my bag and decided there was nothing to do but to forgive him. There was no other way to keep him. There was no other way to love him. It just had to be full of disappointment and love.

Maybe it was just too hard for us, the leavings, so I headed out on that last ferry without saying goodbye but knowing forever where to find him. There was a gray snake of smoke coming from the chimney at Ferry Lands, and I ached only a little.

Thunder

It rattled glass tanks and shook sea animals. I felt it everywhere, too. Jake and I ran around the Sea Institute at night, looking for lightning like we were crazy, and searching for more than love.

Jake was easy to pretend to love. He was from a landlocked place in the middle of the country, surrounded only by faraway rivers that dried up before they found the ocean. His fascination with the Pacific drove his will to live, and he'd been working at the Institute as a research fellow for a few years when he found me mopping up bloody bait leftovers from the faded blue concrete floors. He assumed I was waiting for an opportunity to train a whale.

"Those whales will die in there, you know," I said.

To pay for his tuition, Jake cleaned the glassy tank walls. He mopped, too. He cleaned the cafeteria. Together, we scrubbed the bathrooms in the camp bunks. He smelled like mildew and fish most of the time, and the smell of his ocean rot lingered on my pillows even after vinegar baths. I got used to it. Even his Kentucky accent. Even his hemp necklace.

I was really good at telling myself I was in love with him. That's what I always told him, too. We'd spend days off wandering around the Sea Institute, talking about our dysfunctional parents and dead pets, kissing against windows to jellyfish. He let me stay in his dorm when my mother stopped paying rent and said she'd got an opportunity to sing in a folk band in Nashville. She said it was her dream, and before I could say something like, *Must be so nice to follow your dreams*, she was all packed up and all moved out, and had left a note on a box of pizza that said: *So much love to you and Jake. Keep saving your fish!*

I told Jake I was born near the sea, I'd almost died in the sea, and I was made of more salt than blood. In the early morning sunlight, when Jake awoke next to the tiny window that peered into our small dorm room, I could see a swipe of sun rash on his cheeks, which looked like small holes that had been carved out by shells, and I knew he wouldn't last. He made eggs in a pan on a hot plate and told me that he'd never spent so much time near the ocean, that it made him feel alive, and that one summer, he'd gone to dolphin training camp in Florida, and that's how he knew he was not really born to land.

"You know it's so much colder here than in Florida," he said.

"Can you put cheese on my eggs?" I asked.

Jake was the kind of person who'd studied the history of the Sea Institute and read Jacques Cousteau's entire thesis on Winter Island. He'd seen the Nat Geo specials. He knew that my island was part magic. He treated me like a real celebrity, like my lineage meant something special, like I was special. It was enough to say *love* and pretend to believe it.

"You always wanted a girl from Winter Island," I said.

His pockmarked face crept closer to me. "Always," he said.

The small bed didn't bother either one of us, and we managed to take study turns at the built-in desk. I'd gotten a small promotion, to helping in the lab, not just cleaning, partly because the guy who hired my mom felt terrible she'd left me alone there, and partly because I knew what the fuck I was doing. I was valuable at the Institute. I bore traditional ecological knowledge of my land. I could speak to controlled burns and trophic cascades.

We spent our time with the animals and made obnoxious poetic comparisons to the creatures who mated for life, the ones who ate their young, and then the miraculous seahorse, who could change its sex. Before bed, half-dazed and mostly stoned, we pretended we were animals.

We'd take the skiff and trace the edge of California's coast on hot days. The boat was big enough for kissing but not private enough for fucking.

Our playing love made it easy not to think of my father, imagining him falling down steps, or slamming his truck into a tree. It was easy to forget my mother again, to ignore the hurt, the constant abandonment. But Winter Island lurked nearby, and each morning Jake pointed to the horizon and asked things like, *How can you get lost on an island?*

We spoke of going to Kentucky for Christmas, but the draw to be back on the island, to see if it had eroded in the time passed, was too great. Or, I missed my father. Jake agreed we wouldn't tell my father that we were living together, or that I might stay away forever, or that my mother had evaporated.

DAD WAS WAITING when the ferry locked into the land. I warned him that Jake was my real boyfriend and that he should not make fun of his accent.

"Well, how-dee-doooo-dee, sir. How y'all doing on dis fine daaay?" Dad said.

"Jesus, Dad," I said.

But Jake was already zipping up his jacket and paralyzed by wonder. He said the air smelled different and that it tasted sweet. As we squished into Dad's truck, he grabbed my arm and whispered, *It's all true.*

Dad's face was wind-chapped, because of the time he'd been spending at sea and in the fields. As he pointed out landmarks on the island, he said the tuna were running that year and that he had more tuna in his freezer than he knew what to do with. He was on his best behavior. The car ran smoothly, and he seemed kind of sober. There was no way to tell, when he was being charming.

"Mind if y'all make uh quiiick pit stop before we eat?" Dad said.

Rain beat on the ocean from a family of black clouds. Haze fixed on the horizon. Dad and I knew that it meant a dark storm was coming, one that would knock the power out, close the ferry, and keep Jake with us at least for the night. Dad eyed it in the rearview mirror as we approached the Old Institute. He must have already known it was coming—with all that time at sea and all of his gadgets—and he had let us come anyway. Maybe I had known it was coming, too.

Jake perked up at the hammering of thunder miles away.

"You think there will be snow on top of the volcano?" he asked.

Dad finally stopped talking like what he thought a southerner sounded like and asked me to unlock the chain-link fence into the Old Institute. I could feel that special cold creeping in, and everything, even my eyelashes and the tips of my hair, started to feel damp.

Even though I was gone for a few months, even though it felt like an eternity, I was still proud I remembered the combinations to the locks on the gate.

Dad told us to get out. To explore the old housing tract, to show Jake my grandmother's bunk, to hang out in the dried-up old dolphin pool. He'd be back in a while. Dad vanished into the trees, and Jake looked puzzled, but he ran for the giant map painted on the wall of an old building of classrooms.

"Smells like burgers," he said.

"People still live here," I said.

"What kinds of people?" he asked.

"The kind who never want to leave Winter Island," I said.

He opened and closed doors, bursting in and out of abandoned lives, and he took notes on a pad he kept in his pocket. I sat on the concrete bed frame in our old bunk. I could have told him that this was where I'd spent a few years when Mom left. That we cooked on a barbecue right outside the door and that I had a Paula Abdul poster (which was the exact size of my window) as a curtain. Instead, I let him run his hands along the deteriorating walls while he made jokes about the Old Institute looking just like a mess.

We wandered around the remnants of the decrepit research institute, so much smaller than the giant sea city we now inhabited. The traces of entire families lingered on benches and swings.

I lay down in the dolphin pool and looked up—at the same dark clouds that came every once in a while to remind us that Winter Island wasn't really ours. I drifted off and tried to remember a time I was happy amid the crumbling of our village, and it was most of the time. The sweet air—I'd missed it—was part of me. Jake, wherever he had wandered off to, surely couldn't understand.

"Get this motherfucker out of here," someone shouted.

"Please don't hurt me," Jake yelled.

He called my name over and over, so loudly, and I bolted to the edge of the forest, where two men were holding rifles to his back. His hands were up and if I wanted to be honest, I'd say he peed his pants. He was shaken, in tears, screaming my name.

"Tell them!" he shouted.

They guided him to me with the tips of their guns—both men staring me in the eye and one giving me a wink. I had known those beaten faces my whole life. Leftover guys who watched Dad's pot field in exchange for fish, boat parts, coke, pills, and weed.

"Get him out of here," they said.

Dad honked in the distance, and I grabbed Jake by the hand and ran to the car.

"You know those guys?" he huffed.

"Guards," I said.

"What do they guard?"

"Protected land," I said.

We slid into the truck, and a drizzle painted the window. Dad kept his window down, and Jake rolled his up. Jake was flushed, and choking on quick breaths.

"Like this," I said.

I breathed deeply through my nose and held it, eyes closed, and let it all out of my lungs.

"Y'all are nosy out there in dat darn town of Kentucky, eh?" Dad said.

I glared at my father.

"Now, who wants some real goood fish 'n' chips from Win-tur Island?" Dad asked.

He peeled out. We headed to Rocky's, Jake inhaling deeply with his eyes closed.

In the mirror, I could see that Dad's grow had doubled in size, more than he'd ever had of the greenest Winter Wonderland. I put my hand on Jake's back, and the thunder crept closer.

Jake finally opened his eyes when I begged him to watch the black tunnels of water on the horizon. Dad drove like an outlaw and cheered at the oncoming weather.

"Y'all ain't goin' nowhere tonight," he said.

"Waterspouts out there," I said.

I made small talk about the famous fish-and-chips, which were really fish that were fresh but with everything else from Costco on the mainland. I guided Jake out of the truck before he could see Dad carrying two giant duffel bags stuffed with weed into the office of Rocky's.

When he came back, Dad sat down with a pitcher of beer and told us to drink.

"Hey, how's your mother?" he asked me.

"Light as a feather," I said.

He let out a long yee-haw, and Jake joined in, like they were two wolves crying in the night.

What are your specific qualifications for Lab Research Assistant I? Please explain in a paragraph or less.

(My father and I have grown distant. Our phone calls are bland, and we often talk about my pet fish or whether he's eating enough. I think he's dying.)

Bowhead Whale

Balaena mysticetus

QUESTION: About how many hundreds of years does a bowhead whale live?

Your father will say that someday he'll turn to salt at eventide. That you are to bury him, or set fire to his warm remains, or collect shells and stack them around his body, or whatever the fuck you want to do to him when he's expired. Some days, he'll have preferences about where he wants to disintegrate; some days he'll say things like, *Let me become the air.* You'll shrug, because what else can you do with a man who you believe will live forever.

But he won't live forever. What made you think that? His taut and gold skin? Or his eyes, deep with many lives before you? Was it because he said he'd be here forever? Or that's just what you wanted to believe?

You will have pictured him dying by so many swords, so many different ways—him leaving and never coming back. After all the nights he never came home, he still came back. What about all the times you imagined his head separating from his body, his heart exploding at the sight of a seagull swooping low one of those perfectly warm days. Him just crying to death. He always rose, his lungs full again, and his feet one in front of the other—broken, but there.

Your schoolbooks say that death cannot be prevented. People say to not think of that kind of darkness. That if you see a breathing baby bird fallen from a tree, you cannot save it in a shoebox with soft tissues and toothpicks and love and caution and care. Your father says death will come for you, that everything will come for you, even if you are an island, even if you believe that things last forever. That all of this living forever is tiring.

When your father dies, there will be a pool of blood. He'll die because of a misstep in the dark. A poor calculation of the placing of feet. On the deck of a boat, where there was no light, because your father didn't replace the bulbs after a storm.

But that storm had always been coming. Him sinking, him shriveling up, choking, laughing so hard. You'd like to imagine him as old as the oldest whale, weathered and ready to drop to the bottom after all the years a body can carry. You've always been preparing for this death, before you realized that he'd just be gone forever. Believing that one day, when you are annoyed that there isn't any cream left for the coffee, you'll get the news that it's over.

You will guess he'd wanted his death to be more romantic than a drunkard falling in total darkness. Hoped that his passing from one island to another wouldn't be covered in blood; that maybe there'd be some romance, some kind of ocean monster taking him whole, some kind of end-of-the-world sunset to take him home. But by the time they find him, there will be blood everywhere. His head slammed against the side of the boat so hard it nearly split him in two. Maybe that part is sweet. They'll let you see the star-shaped stains on the deck. They'll say it will take for-ever to make clean again.

There will be some shock and some relief, too, because do you have to worry about someone who isn't yours any-more? When you get the call, you'll be lying on your back, on a bed that's not yours in a little bedroom on the main-land, dreaming of Winter Island, quietly worrying about everything, but still happy to be away from him.

When you hear they've found a body, that space between you and him will be the pressure of all the oceans on Earth. You'll say sorry to the captain on the phone, like you knew this would happen, like it was your fault. It'll be the only time in your life you say what you mean out loud: *Wait, is he coming back?*

You're sorry for everyone, even yourself. For him, too, because no one was there to hear his last gurgles of blood. Because no one was there to fix him. To force him to quit the bad things. To tell him to stop. To tell you to lock him in a cage.

In a letter, the state of California will explain that he bled to death after smashing his brains apart. That he was so goddamn wasted out at sea that his blood alco-hol level was thrice the legal limit. They imagine that he woke up to piss off the side of the boat, a dream you replay in your mind for the rest of your nights. They say you will never know if he tripped, or slipped, or—damn it—slammed his own fucking head into the bluntness of the bow.

Your father was wearing a long-sleeved shirt with loose-fitting boxers when he died, they say. You can have his clothes, but they say that sometimes people shit themselves when they die, so you'll say you don't want them. You won't want any of it.

You'll know that he ate onions, because they are in the gray matter of his stomach. And beer. And THC. And just about everything else. He had bloody knuckles when he died. That poor coroner tried to piece them together with stories of violent sea hooks and storms, but you'll know those bloody hands were traces of other men's faces and noses and ribs. You'll keep replaying his few steps to the end, rocking out there at sea, and you'll imagine him as he always was when he stumbled home: with one eye open.

You won't be able to help but think of the times he never came home, before you left for the mainland, when you knew he was somewhere out there, breathing and surviving. He could get by on very little. He always said the important things were deep inside him, protected by a rib cage, and that once he vanished, you'd always be able to find him there.

For years, you'll keep asking, *Where?* Until the day you dump his ashes overboard, because there is no money to bury him on Winter Island, and you hope that he won't be lost at sea forever but that he'll fall to the bottom, where an entire universe can form around what's left of him. The rest of him, you guess, is somewhere inside you now.

Some nights, when your father returned after long days, he'd bring a gift. A peace offering. A seashell. A magazine. A doughnut. A bag of gummy worms. A kitten that you'd have to give away. A hula girl for the dash. A necklace that would turn your neck green. He'd never say sorry, and you'd never ask him to. Sometimes, your anger felt like nothing, and sometimes, everything. All the time you pretended it never happened. Because you loved him and he loved you, and there was no time to waste, because you must have known that it was unlikely that your father would live forever.

You'll keep dreaming of him each night after he's gone. For a long time in those dreams, he hides from you—pretends you are not his—and then, finally, he appears from behind curtains, frightened to see you. Sometimes in your dreams, you'll scream at him. Sometimes, you'll wake to your own tears. You'll replay your father walking in the night to the bow of that boat, until you fall asleep, and you dream again.

There he is, in his loose-fitting clothes, and there's a breeze and maybe some moonlight. And it's not him pissing off the boat; it's him waking to the sound of a whale calling to him. The sound of air pushing through water. You'll dream he died chasing wonder. And eventually, he gracefully dives off the tip of the boat, and you can see him there floating on top of the Earth.

In some of those dreams, you jump with him.

Wildfire

The late-summer wildfires had scorched all the way to the beach, and the Santa Monica Mountains were bleeding soot. Winter Island was the only place that wasn't on fire. And on my trips back and forth, I checked in on my father, whose hair was thinning, whose skin was not so tight. I'd bring green juices from LA health-food stores, force him to drink them, bring him dates and salad. The doctors told him he'd have to give up the hard stuff if he wanted to last much longer. So he cut back on the coke and focused on whiskey and joints.

Before I'd go back to my life on the mainland, he'd ask about my mother. He never stopped asking. There were postcards from Paris on his fridge.

"She's gone again," I said.

"I know it."

We had a routine: he'd put the weed into my bag, Mary let me on the ferry, and I'd sell it as fast as I could in LA. I'd wait until I got to my room at the Sea Institute to unravel the Winter Wonderland. *Charge those LA fuckers extra*, a note said. I spent my mornings working in the lab, and afternoons selling Baggies of weed to students, faculty, and nearby Starbucks employees for cash. Within a few weeks, I'd get back on the ferry, my bag full of twenties, and chat with Mary about stars, Ferry Lands, cats, cows, fathers, disappointments, dinosaurs, and anything else we could think up.

WHAT HAD MY mother told me about forgiveness?

I SHOULDN'T HAVE been surprised when Rook suddenly appeared at my door, disheveled and sweaty, and demanding that she'd have to stay in my room for a while. Her marriage to some French guy hadn't worked out, and she'd been hiding on Winter Island for months while I'd believed she was wearing berets in Paris. I tucked away this small betrayal, the one about her not telling me she was home, but knew that our friendship had suffered plenty of time and distance already. She said she was restless on the island, and that my father convinced her to bring over another full bag of Wonderland. She unzipped the bag from my father, just as neatly packed as always, took a green pinch for herself, and sprinkled it into a small rolling paper.

I wanted to say: *How is my father? I don't want you to see him. I don't want to see him, either. I don't know why you came here.*

MY MOTHER SAID it was impossible to forgive people. Because a betrayal happens to you right in the gut. That you can't just forget the jellyfish that stopped your heart.

"YOU CAN'T SMOKE weed in here," I said.

"Is this a real college?" she asked.

"I could really lose my job," I said.

She lay on my bed, her feet up the wall, messing up my blankets, and kept saying things like, *You're so borrrriing now* and *Let's fucking go ouuut.* She danced around in my white lab coat, and opened and closed the flaps like she was flashing her tits. She put on lipstick in the tiny mirror of my shower caddy. She said she knew some guys in Hollywood; she said she'd promised Dad to show me how to get more money for the weed. I wanted to know how much time she'd spent with my father, if she loved him, if she knew whether everything would be all right.

Rook didn't want to talk about her failed marriage. She didn't want to talk about anything except how badly she needed a night out. How boring the island was.

"How can anyone live there for so long?" she said.

She looked young and beautiful, especially in lipstick, and it was so easy for me to love people who loved only themselves. She moved my things around and scribbled doodles on my lab worksheets. We sat on a bench in the courtyard and smoked cigarettes, and sipped whiskey from airplane bottles from her purse.

We toured the dolphins, the sea otters, the jellyfish, the swarming schools of silver fish, the aviary. She leaked a few tears at the flapping of wings, and she said it was the fact that they were caged that made her so sad. But her tears became deep stains of mascara and I knew there was more.

The thing about me and Rook was that we didn't push each other to talk about the things we didn't want to talk about, but in case we did, we knew we'd be there to listen. We pressed our backs into the great lawn of the Institute, and the sun was lost. It was dark enough, and I was buzzed enough, that I said we could smoke a J while we waited for the stars.

"I think I'm pregnant," she said.

She said she wasn't sure about the father, or whether she was keeping it, whether she was sure of anything. She still hadn't decided, and she wanted to keep walking. She spoke as if she were consoling me.

She kissed me on the forehead, and we locked pinkies as we climbed to the top of a lighthouse. There was the top of Winter Island, like a man dead on his back, lying right in the water. We could see the whole island from end to end. She screamed out, a wild and wicked squeal, and laughed at the rumble of her echo. We slumped our backs against the concrete walls and cool tile floor, and the wind whipped.

She laughed until she cried again and put her head in her hands. I leaned my head against her shoulder. She took my hand to her belly and pressed it deep into her skin. We felt nothing.

We talked about being alone, its glory and its darkness, and then she said she'd been in love with another man for a long time. I said we could make an appointment and get it all fixed, that we'd have enough weed money to get rid of the baby, or keep it—whatever Rook needed to be happy.

"I just want to be here tonight," she said.

"Okay."

WHAT HAD MY mother told me about happiness?

WHEN WE GOT to Hollywood, we were both all black-and-red lips, with clunky tall shoes and bare legs. Rook's friends got us into the bar through a back door, and she drank like she never wanted to wake up.

"Maybe I'll move to the mountains," she said.

I hated her for saying it.

Then there was broken glass and yelling, and it was Rook's guys, and she pulled me out of that place so fast that it seemed the back of my neck was sore from being carried by a mother cat.

We wandered around Hollywood Boulevard and pretended we were brave. We couldn't be lonely when we were together, even if we were just drunkenly selling too-cheap weed to homeless people and tourists.

A limo appeared in front of Grauman's Chinese Theatre, and a drunk bachelor party filed out to take photos with fake celebrities and a less red, dingy version of Elmo. Soon, we were inside the limo, and a hand was up Rook's skirt. *Will it hurt the baby?* I kept yelling in my head. I was asleep on a married man's shoulder after I told him about intertidal ecology. When they dropped us off at the Institute, most of the weed was gone, and we couldn't remember what we'd sold, given away, or smoked ourselves.

Rook and I squeezed into my dorm bed, and it was the first time I'd gone to sleep without the blue light of the TV.

In the morning, Rook was gone, and she'd left a note that said she'd taken the money back to Dad. I aimlessly wandered around the grounds that day—a Sunday, when most people were gone—and found myself following the sounds of birds singing mysteriously pleasant songs against netting woven together, which made an enormous cage.

My MOTHER SAID that happiness was like flying.

Breeze

I could see for miles. Gentle winds made a clear, sunshiny horizon. The whale breaths. Fish that flew. Sinking ships. I heard it might never be this clear again. I hiked to the top of the volcano, and up there was the rest of the world. Below, my father, his son, and perfectly manicured rows of marijuana. Everything was endless.

He sat on Dad's lap—the exact same back-of-the-head hair. They were fishing in the little pond in the middle of the weed field. When they turned to me, I wanted to yell, to scratch Dad's eyes out for all the lies, but it was so quiet and cool, and the pond water erupted silent bubbles to the surface. Tommy roared with laughter at the deep voices of frogs hidden under tall grass and moss. They pushed their poles into the earth, and my father smiled.

"You haven't met Tommy yet," Dad said.

He was three. A perfect little face and a sweeter disposition than Dad or I ever had. I was a rough kid, quiet, alone, pondering and wondering. But Tommy was happy, loud, excited. All the things I wanted to be. We shook hands. Tommy's palm was a tiny, greasy thing, covered in dried mud.

"Top of the morning to you, Tom," I said.

"Tommy!" he shouted.

He ran back to his pole and dunked his feet into the pond. Dad watched him out of the side of his eye. It smelled like weed, and my father smiled. It wasn't the time to bring up the past, the deceit, the money he'd borrowed, the promises he'd broken.

"Rook's gone, then?" I asked.

He nodded. Sad and old.

He never told me that Tommy was his, but it seems like everyone knew, including him, so we never did have to talk about it. I didn't want the details about how Rook had been sleeping with Dad the whole time I was gone—probably the whole time before that, too.

I knew he'd gotten her a job waiting tables at Otto House. I knew he went there every night after Rocky's. I knew these things but never found the right words to say anything. To ask him about it was to allow him to ask me how I felt about it. We were the kind of people who had to be quiet to move on with things. Talking it all out would have fractured us forever.

"Ice cream," Tommy yelled.

In the distance, my father's broken-down truck sat on the edge of what was left of the Old Institute. It was the last of any of the outside world that bothered to come anymore. Tommy clapped his hands and jumped—his feet squishing in and out of the mud. The guys with guns whistled to Dad.

"Watch him, would you?" he said to me.

I cupped a tiny frog in my hands and opened them slowly. Tommy giggled and reached.

"Be gentle," I said.

He ripped it from my hands and squeezed hard, and the frog slipped out and into the green.

"More," he said.

The top half of his face, and especially his wavy hair, looked just like Dad. And his smirk was all Rook. He didn't get her ruby-colored lips, though.

I wanted to dislike this little boy, but when he grabbed my hand and led me into a muggy sanctuary of frog noises and puddle smells, I knew that he was part of us. We had the same eyes, as if his were mine and mine were his, and I hoped I had once been so full of wonder as he was. And I'd been hoping for things to keep for so long, although I felt like everything was always cracking and sinking, that I had learned to love despair even in sunlight. When Tommy turned to me with his eyes wide, telling me about bugs, I kept asking the same question: *What if I could love someone despite betrayal?*

After everything else we'd endured, it seemed useless to rage-scream at my father, or to scold Rook. And here was this new little body of a boy, with hope, stamping his feet into soft ground, asking me if I'd stay and pluck tadpoles out of still water. Maybe I needed him most.

Tommy couldn't spend any more time in those sweltering-by-day and freezing-by-night barracks. For the sake of myself, for Tommy, and Dad, and the miles of things we were finally able to see, I had to stay. Forever.

THEN DAD GOT an apartment big enough for three. Near the old butcher shop, so that sometimes smells of metallic meat and old, bloodied bones wafted through the living room. If I stood on a stool in the bathtub and stretched my neck out the window, I could see a tiny glimmer of the sea. That season, we could always see the foreverness of ocean. Depending on the time of day, it was an endless green or blue or purple. The plumbing was bad and the floors creaked, but that place was well worth the afternoon breeze. From the roof, we could see for miles.

Dad said that Tommy wouldn't remember the mainland or Rook or the rains or the heat, or anything else that happened before now. I think we were all ready to forget a few hundred of our mistakes by then and focus on what to eat for dinner. On raising a boy.

"Fresh lobster," Dad said.

All the storms had left my father tired. There was a small patch of yard where we grew fresh herbs, radishes, carrots, and peppers. Dad also grew tomatoes and cared for them with a gentle hand. His expertise in weed farming had translated into an old-man hobby, and by then, he was growing most of our food himself.

He'd lost the whole operation to crooks, and whatever was left, people came for it, and demanded he pay debts. He gambled anything else that was left at an Indian casino in the desert. The last few wads of cash were spent on quality steaks for the grill. People approached us about licensing the name, or making a movie about us, or asking us for the mother seed, but Dad never responded.

Those days were quiet. Dad worked on the yard and on fixing our old garage door and splintery steps. He drank less and looked forward to watching Tommy play submarines in the bathtub. He followed new recipes. We walked for miles. Tommy fell asleep in a fancy stroller sent by Rook's parents.

Dad bundled Tommy in a snowsuit, a puffy onesie he'd received from Rook when she was waiting tables in Aspen. He appeared in the doorway, already sweaty, holding Dad's hand.

"Tin Pan is reporting a big lobster day," Dad said.

"Can Tommy swim?" I asked.

THERE WERE STILL a few hours of warmth, and we could see on and on, and Dad said the Earth *looked* round. There was a most pleasant breeze and I grabbed a bag full of snacks and water, in case we'd be stuck out there forever and ever. Some kind of motherly instinct had taken over, though I'd never had a mother, or been a mother, or wanted to be one. But the small army of people and the endless loop of Winter Island seemed to have performed some kind of magic trick: I could love unconditionally. Even still. After hating my father. And my mother. And Rook. And sometimes myself.

The fishing boat was the only thing that was really Dad's, and it was tattered but functional, painted with a faded, horrific shade of coral that he said reminded him of the color of his mother's apron.

Tin Pan glowed in the late afternoon, and we quietly slipped out of the harbor's mouth. Tommy clapped at the seagulls shouting, and I held him so close, nearly pressing his life vest into my skin. I wasn't a mother, but I was a mother. I wasn't a daughter, but I was a daughter.

"You have to let him live a little," Dad said.

"Maybe I shouldn't take parenting advice from you," I said.

Looking up from his rusted lobster pots, Dad scowled.

"You don't seem so miserable being back here," he said.

What if loving them didn't make me miserable? What if I was happy even if nothing would be perfect.

TOMMY POINTED TO anything that moved, and on the horizon, the whale-watching boats, packed tightly with tourists, were coming in for the day. Then there was the buoy with shiny black sea lions yelping as we passed, the same buoy Dad said I screamed at, too. Tommy told us to *look and look and look.*

"You can see the rest of the Channel Islands out there," Dad said.

"You remember when you told tourists that was Japan?" I asked.

Dad anchored, and we dropped three pots, hoping for at least one lobster. But as we sat there waiting, Dad shuffling cards and Tommy watching, I think I must have forgotten why we were resting on top of the sea that afternoon. We ate crackers and all sipped water from Tommy's baby cup. Tommy was loud, and obnoxious, and joyous, and for a moment, there was hope.

"I hope you're not sad it ended up this way," Dad said.

"Which way?" I asked.

"The way it was supposed to be," he said.

I couldn't tell him, right on the boat, that, no, he shouldn't have fucked my friend, and then betrayed me, and her, that then there was Tommy, and what? We would just endure another round of suffering? I couldn't, because there was this: my father, happy, with peaceful eyes.

We played War and enjoyed an eerily calm day at sea. When he pulled the lobster pots from the seafloor, Tommy squealed in excitement. We'd have enough for a week.

"Look at this big guy!" Dad said.

We coasted back to the dock, Dad pointing out new neighbors, new shops, new boats, and all the things he knew about the island's future. His voice was older. The dock was decrepit and should have been torn down after the last hurricane, but Dad swore it would last another summer.

Tommy helped Dad carry the cooler, stocked full of slow-moving lobster, and I packed up the life vests and tied the boat properly for the night.

But that damn rickety dock was too unstable for Tommy, and within seconds, he tripped right into the sea. The sound of his body crashing into the dirty pool of shallow green water sent small pains to every sensor in my body. Like he was mine.

Dad had him by the arm and out of the water, plopped down on the dock, was consoling Tommy's screams, before I could even get out of the boat.

"What the fuck do you think you're doing?" I screamed.

I grabbed Tommy, covering him in all my dry coats and scarves and ran him back to the apartment. I never once looked back to see if Dad was behind me. Tommy's lips were blue from the late-afternoon wind, and his screams—thank god for his screams—were hearty and real.

I stripped him down and plunked him in the bathtub with warm water, and I could hear Dad eventually building a fire in the living room. Tommy played with submarines, as if his near drowning had occurred in another life, as if those kinds of things didn't happen on Winter Island.

In the kitchen, I heard pots clanking and the fire crackling loudly. I heard the sound of a fast knife on the cutting board, the refrigerator door squeaking open and the steam scream of the boiled lobster in the pot. Dad did the actual boiling of the lobster because I couldn't bear a loud death. I wrapped Tommy in a warm robe and we sat by the fire, bundled up, full of warmth.

When we ate dinner, we ate in silence, only speaking to Tommy and entertaining his jokes.

"That happened to you, you know?" Dad said.

I made faces at Tommy.

"You fell in so many times," Dad said.

"Let me guess, I saved myself?" I said.

"I saved you many times."

DAD DUTIFULLY DID the dishes after we ate, and we watched cartoons on the couch until all three of us, full and quiet, were falling asleep next to the fire. I could smell fall creeping through the curtains, and it roared in from the shore.

That night, there wasn't a dream without dark-green water, mysterious islands, sea monsters with shiny black skin, and coral-colored winds that brought some courage and understanding.

Blue Whale

Balaenoptera musculus

QUESTION: Which whale has the largest heart of any known animal?

Your father will tell you that your ribs are the same as a whale's. A rounded, white, brittle cage that holds all the moving things inside you. *That's where your heart goes*, he'll say, and he'll put his hand on top of his chest, and count off the beats with a funny drum sound he makes between his lips. *Listen for it*, he'll say. *Even if it doesn't keep on beating*, he'll say.

When he tells you this for the first time, you are too young; you are rolling around in the sand, and you believe that you are actually made of seawater and that there are tiny creatures living inside the safety of your rib cage. How could you know that he's telling you where love lives?

When your father tells you that your heart is the size of a blue whale's, he'll point to the horizon, he'll smile, he'll look just like him, he'll be happy. He'll say you don't have to see it to know how it feels to have a heart like that. *Four hundred pounds*, he'll say. He'll tell you that, like his, your heart will sometimes ache as if it will explode, and that sometimes joy can kill you, too. Everything can kill you, is what he's saying, but you won't be listening. He's telling you he hopes you'll be wild enough to love things you cannot see.

He will tell you to be careful. Accidentally, he will tell you to build walls without telling you to build them. Over the years, you will watch his heart ache and sing and burn out. And then do it again, and again. He will tell you that once he goes, just like the sun sinks to the bottom of the ocean, you will just look inside your own body of swimming things, inside your own giant inherited heart, and he'll be there. *Forever*, he'll say. Because not everything dissolves in water.

And he will show you that most things hurt and that you don't have to talk about them, but that if you seal yourself up to your deepest depth, your heart will shrink. It will beat slow, and low, and the light will go out. That joy will not find you unless your blood is pumping. He'll say we are all made of the same salt water, our hearts too big, even if they seem so small. He'll say we'll always just miss each other, even when we are sitting shoulder-to-shoulder on the sand.

Your father will tell you all of this when you are too young, when you are plucking starfish from sticky rocks. When the seagulls are loud. He'll say his love for you is infinite, unexplainable like the things above and below, that his love for you could kill him. You will hug him, because you're just a kid, and you'll laugh at how much he loves you. You'll imagine that everyone will love you this way, because what else could there be?

While you're wrestling a starfish off of the palm of your hand, he will tell you to love even the things you can't see.

He'll say to believe in the things that aren't always shown in the light. You won't care about this then. He'll say it's like when a devil ray swims right over your head. He'll make a whoosh sound. He'll spread his arms like an eagle. You'll never see a devil ray, but you know it's there, always lurking, and, goddamn it, it's a real fish.

So your father will spend years telling you that when he's gone, he'll always be right there with you—except how can you know what that means? He's been letting you run around a beach without any sunscreen, with no hat; he's lost your shoes. How can you know what it's like to lose the people you love when you are still trying to figure out how to love them? He will keep saying it—there's a fish or a bird for it, every time, on every day. He'll keep saying he knows that things just keep moving, and keep living, that they do it with him and will do it without him.

Then your father will take you the long way to the lost beach, with the whale carcass that has washed onto the shore. You'll hike through the dunes, and you'll dunk your hands into the coolness of morning sand and pull purple shells and shove them in your pockets. You won't be able to believe the wretchedness of that whale odor, but your father will make you walk right up to the body—your first dead body. He won't let you poke it with a stick. He won't let you throw a rock at it. He'll tell you not to plug your nose, that it's rude, and then he will explain the process of a whale rotting. How it will become nothing and, also, part of everything.

He'll take you to this whale each day, on the long hike to the shore, and you'll always remember the curve of its body so vividly, the roundness of its eye. Eventually, the whale will have been picked apart by birds, unruly kids, and everything else, and your father will wait until night to steal the bones, the fullness of ribs.

He'll take those giant bones to every single home you make together, even the ones in the woods, until finally, your father, too, is just a carcass working to dissolve in the saltiness of ocean, and you're the one now stuck with no father, and with a few enormous tooth-white ribs that once protected a giant heart.

You will miss your father so hard, and all the things that have left, even some of the things that come back. You will lie on your back, looking at the sky, and count your own human ribs with your fingertips, until you can feel him again, until there is a tide rising in your chest, until, like he always said, he is not gone.

SUNDAY

On Sunday, we spend the day waiting for night. My mother and I can easily avoid the shame of our hangovers, the rottenness, the uneasiness of Liam's missing boat, and the very dead whale. A few local vendors stop in with wedding things, and I direct them around Ferry Lands. My mother bakes a cake and says it's a groom's cake. It's the shape of an odd fish, and she says it's kind of the shape of Winter Island. I nap in a hammock. The dogs bark at the trucks that go up and down the driveway. Someone sets up rows of chairs. We play Monopoly. My mother combs my hair. We eat whatever we can find and force ourselves to drink a lot of water. We check the clocks, hoping for the quickness of dark, before our courage escapes, before we can't do any of it, before my mother wants to leave. We say nothing. We must sleep as much as we can, before the darkest of night calls.

My mother finds me on the lawn, with the dogs, reading a book, and waiting. She tells me there was a phone call, that a few boats are returning today and tomorrow, no reports of any damage. There is no one missing. I want to cry, leap into her arms, tell her that I'm happy that Liam will come back to me. I want to tell her that I was worried he'd leave me forever. Exactly the way she did. Exactly the way everything does. *It's science,* I want to say.

"I'm sorry," she says.

"For what?" I say.

"For everything," she says.

She says we should walk, because it will make us feel better. She starts to explain all the reasons she's left—something about the wind, and that urge for going—and I tell her to stop. That I know she's sorry and that I don't want to talk about it. I tell her there's no need to do it anymore. That there's not much left anyway, and I want to enjoy the wedding. And her. And my life.

"I don't even smell that whale anymore," I say.

She nods.

The whale's rolled onto her side, and she's propped up on a low-tide sandbar. There are scabs exposed, and birds, and the body looks like it's not a body at all, but a gray mountain emerging from the sea. She asks why it won't recede. Why nature just won't take care of the whale on its own. Why the Sea Institute hasn't come to deal with the mess.

"They can't get a tow in time," I say.

We examine the hump of whale blubber from the shore, and the dogs follow as we walk down the beach. I say I'm worried about sharks. About sea lions. My mother holds my hand, and I pull away. I remember my heart, and the water that surrounds it.

"I can really smell it now," she says.

We dip our feet into a thick carpet of ocean foam and sink our hands into holes filled with water. We touch the roughness of red and orange sea stars, and my mother gently pokes the center of an anemone with a stick. She collects shells and puts them in her pockets. The dogs are wet and shaking water onto our pants, and I can't help but gaze past the rotted whale to the line of fishing boats that are far away but close enough to really see them.

We keep waiting for darkness.

MY MOTHER IS sleeping on the porch swing, and her face is in the sun. A breeze rocks the swing. There is a smile on her face, or a squint. I creep into the space next to her, and she knows I'm there and leans in closer, and I lay my head next to hers, and we keep rocking. I whisper to her that the boats are coming in. That we should eat a big dinner, because I'll need her to swim tonight.

"I'm not swimming with that fucking whale," she says.

"It's the only way," I say.

I say I don't want to cook, that I don't want to dirty any more dishes before the guests arrive tomorrow. That I can see a squall on the horizon—there are clouds thick with darkness—and that I can't look out there anymore, that I need to get away, that I need to waste time, that we need to get dinner somewhere else.

The dogs get a bowl of dry food, and we drive to get a pizza from a restaurant at the harbor. The whole town is lined with tourists, wasted on weekend getaways. My mother parks in front of a bar with a big patio and a live band. She eats a slice right from the box and grabs a roll of paper towels she's stashed in her purse. She tells me that most women wouldn't eat pizza before their wedding night, but that *we* aren't most women.

"That drummer really liked you last night," she says, staring at the bar band.

I laugh and keep eating.

"You can have anything you want," she says.

My mother gets like this: worried that she's fucked me up so bad that I can't love the right way. And for once, I say something I really mean: *I have what I want.*

Then the darkness comes in waves of violet, and the streetlamps are lit. She asks me about the whales. About my work. About the years of research. She says she's sorry for missing my lectures, awards, and readings on the mainland. Says she never had anything to say to the people at the Sea

Institute. She talks of my father, and Rook, and Liam, and then, of all the other people that we've lost to the sea and the sky.

Nothing else matters anymore. We smoke a joint and drive slowly, dodging gangs of drunk tourists, and we reach the edge of Ferry Lands, where the lighthouse strobe bounces off the statue of Saint Francis of Paola, and my mother says, *It's impossible not to love this place.* We are high on the new pot that comes from labs on the mainland, pizza, and what we think must be forgiveness. We waste time. She reads aloud. She sips wine; I sip wedding champagne. We drift off, and wake up, and tell ourselves we need the sleep.

SHE WAKES ME at four, and it's the darkest part of the early morning night. There is just enough time. My mother borrows an old wet suit and a blue hooded raincoat. We are both zipped up in rubber, waterproofed. Our hair is pulled back. At night, we could be the same woman with a sleek ponytail. We are thankful for the almost-full moon, its light that will guide us out to sea and back again.

We take the dinghy out, with oars only in the closeness of the bay, because the motor could wake any distant neighbor. Island neighbors are nosy when we break laws. We avoid the light and are quiet as we push it into the water, the hull cutting wet sand like a dull knife. We row in unison, my mother quietly following my lead, and we glide toward the body of the whale. At first, I count the times I dig my oar into the sea, like I would count the steps up a staircase, and then I lose count, because it's dark, it's quiet, and the paddle out feels never-ending.

When we are close enough, I place my oar in the water, pushing backward to break our momentum. My mother carefully lowers the anchor into the water, and we wait for the tug that tells us it's hit bottom. She feeds it slowly, making as little noise as a chain-link rope can make while diving into the dark sea against a tin boat. It's almost impossible to be quiet in a boat with water lapping and sloshing all around. *Perhaps now*, she whispers, *we are far enough from land.*

We are moving now without words, using only gestures, and it's the silence, more than the rancid smell, that is most alarming. Perhaps we have never been this still, this efficient, this careful, together. I keep my mouth shut.

We slip into the sea, and I am overcome by the deep darkness below. Its nothingness and everythingness all under my feet is a cocoon for our bodies. We swim around the whale, the waves in the distance sounding like other whales, and we reach her massive nicked fluke. We kick our legs with vigor underwater, but ease cautiously with our arms and hands, like spoons. She's rotted now, her eyes pecked out. She has open sores. Still, no creature has halved her body or taken her whole, so there is the rigorous process of tying rope to the smallest part of her fluke. We are careful, as if she is alive. We quietly agree that beneath leftover moonlight, we will do this with stillness. With dignity.

We touch her. We have already forgotten the stench. She creaks and rocks, and we get the rope fastened to her tail. I keep my mouth closed.

My mother swims to the boat first. I am slower, tugging the rope back like a leash. We sketched it out the night before on napkins at the bar, after we fought for hours about the best way to get rid of a rotting whale, and this plan, the one we agreed upon, was all that was left. We weighed the risks—sharks and more—but this creature was begging for her freedom. And I know the way of water.

My mother helps me back into the boat, and the whale is pulling away with the tide. We'd planned to have many extra feet for give, but when the wind picks up, there's not as much as we'd hoped. I hold the whale like a dead dog on a leash while my mother is whispering, *Hurryhurryhurry.*

In the boat, we breathe heavily and we try to rest. Our rubber suits keep our hearts warm, but our wet hair, helmets of cold, grows colder as the minutes pass. I tug the rope to make sure we're still attached, and my mother hands me an oar. I lift the anchor. We row. She's keeping track of time, and my mother keeps saying we need to go harder, faster, if we want to get this whale out with the help of the tide.

With some momentum, we are slowly dragging this thing out to sea. When we pass the wide mouth of the bay, the jetty, when our arms are burning, my mother says it's time for the motor.

"This is how all women should spend the night before their wedding," she whispers.

WITH THE MOTOR, our wet hair, and the wind in our aching ears, we speed out toward the horizon. We go until we think we've gone too far. *The sun could be coming soon,* she says, looking at her watch. The whale is not far behind.

When we stop, we are panting and we must try to breathe. We move slowly still, just in case, and we get her so far out there. I'm the one who cuts the rope. We watch her slowly float away. She'll be devoured by daylight, we say. Or sunk. But not gone.

My mother opens a canvas bag full of roses. She has picked every color, and she hands them to me by their long stems. In the almost-light, we cannot see the thorns and our hands are too cold to feel them. We quickly pull the petals and pile them in the base of the hull, and we are silent and we are peaceful. Then we take them by the handful and sprinkle them onto the sea, and they float toward the whale until they all begin to separate and move and go their own way. We are letting go of everything.

Our boat is tossed around, and we rush back into the safety of the bay with our motor, cut it, row back over the sandbars, and then, there is the shore. Altogether, it could have been a few minutes or one full lifetime.

We unzip one another and rinse thoroughly in the outside shower. The water is nearly warm, and the sun, nearly awake. I ask my mother if she wants coffee, while we shiver under the same trickle of water, whale smell all over.

"You should really get some sleep," she says.

She offers to pull in the boat, wash it down, prepare for the rest of the day. She says she has floral arrangements to make.

For a moment, we stare at the horizon and try to find our whale, but already she's too far gone and we can no longer smell anything foul over the morning dew on flowers and this rising tide.

Conclusion:

What fills the space: everything we have lost and found.